ANIMAL RESCUE TEAM

Hide
and
Seek

SUE STAUFFACHER

ANIMAL RESCUE TEAM

Hide
and
Seek

illustrated by
PRISCILLA LAMONT

Alfred A. Knopf ⟶ New York

THIS IS A BORZOI BOOK PUBLISHED BY ALFRED A. KNOPF

All rights reserved. Published in the United States by Alfred A. Knopf, an imprint of Random House Children's Books, a division of Random House, Inc., New York.

Knopf, Borzoi Books, and the colophon are registered trademarks of Random House, Inc.

Visit us on the Web! www.randomhouse.com/kids

Educators and librarians, for a variety of teaching tools, visit us at www.randomhouse.com/teachers

Library of Congress Cataloging-in-Publication Data
Stauffacher, Sue.
Hide and seek / Sue Stauffacher ; illustrated by Priscilla Lamont. — 1st ed.
   p.   cm. — (Animal rescue team)
Summary: The Carter family's Halloween preparations are complicated by a deer with a pumpkin stuck on its head and a puppy that is part dog, part coyote.
ISBN 978-0-375-85849-9 (trade) — ISBN 978-0-375-95849-6 (lib. bdg.) —
ISBN 978-0-375-89704-7 (e-book)
[1. Halloween—Fiction. 2. Deer—Fiction. 3. Dogs—Fiction. 4. Animal rescue—Fiction. 5. Wildlife rescue—Fiction. 6. Family life—Fiction. 7. Racially mixed people—Fiction.] I. Lamont, Priscilla, ill. II. Title.
PZ7.S8055Tri 2010
[Fic]—dc22
2009040073

The text of this book is set in 13-point Goudy.

Printed in the United States of America
September 2010
10 9 8 7 6 5 4 3 2 1

First Edition

In memory of our dear friend Scott "Pritch" Pritchett
(1961–2009), whose smile lit up the room

*A smile costs nothing but gives much. It enriches those who
receive it without making poorer those who give. It takes but a
moment, but the memory of it can last forever.*
—Anonymous

Chapter 1

Keisha Carter set out five pieces of bread and buttered them. Using a biscuit cutter, she made a hole in the center of each piece and settled them butter-side-down into Daddy's hot pan.

"Please get Grandma the ice pack from the freezer," Daddy said as he cracked eggs into the empty spaces.

Keisha stood on her tippy-toes and felt for the ice pack. "Did she have yoga last night?"

"Yes. According to Bob, she was showing their instructor the new move she's made up. Cat-falling-off-counter or something like that. She strained her back a little."

Big Bob, as all the kids called him, worked as a vet tech at the Humane Society, was the leader of their 4-H's Wild 4-Ever Club and always put his yoga mat next to Grandma's at Yoga You Can Do. But he was *not* Grandma's boyfriend.

"Take it right up and ask her if she wants breakfast in bed. And please find Razi for me. You don't want to be late for school. Tell him I'm making toad-in-the-hole. That'll get him going."

As Keisha hurried down the hall, she heard the phone ringing in the office. Grandma usually answered the phone on school mornings, but she was upstairs groaning.

"I'll get it," Keisha called back to Daddy in the kitchen, so he didn't have to leave the eggs. "Carters' Urban Rescue," she answered, a little out of breath.

"Oh dear. Oh, the poor little deer."

"Excuse me?" Keisha asked.

"I have a deer here that needs rescuing."

"Do you live in the city?" Though the Carters had rescued a lot of animals since they set up their business, it wasn't often they got a call about a deer.

"I should think so. I'm right on the edge of Huff Park."

Huff Park was less than a mile from the Carters' home.

"Is the deer injured?" Keisha sat down at the desk and opened the "animal info" file drawer. She yanked out the file labeled "deer."

"Well, no. Not precisely . . . Good heavens, look at the time! I'll miss my bus."

Keisha felt her stomach grumbling. "If the deer isn't injured, why does it need to be rescued?" she asked, hoping to hurry the call to an end for the lady who was about to miss her bus *and* for her empty stomach.

"Because he can't get the pumpkin off his head!"

Keisha was so surprised, she didn't know what to say.

"Hello? Did you hear me? If I miss the 7:42, I'll be late for work. And I'm the one who makes the coffee. Dr. Trimble says it is the only civilized cup of coffee he gets in a day."

Keisha did not know the difference between civilized coffee and uncivilized coffee, but in the end they were supposed to be talking about a deer, weren't they?

"About the deer . . . ," Keisha prompted.

"I live at 422 Joan Street. The street dead-ends at the park. In a few months, we'll have cross-country skiers trampling my perennial beds. I'm looking out my back door right now and he's . . . he's taking the trail that leads to the baseball diamonds. Oh, the poor deer. How will he eat? How will he drink? Please come out and get this pumpkin off his head."

"But how did he get—"

"Every Halloween time, I put it out for birds with

the seeds right in it. He must have been after the salt on the seeds, poor thing, and it got stuck on his head. There's nothing I can do about it now, and being late for work and having Mary Nell make the coffee won't help the deer's plight. I just don't understand why it's stuck so fast. Isn't there *something* you can do?"

"Well, I can tell my dad—"

"Your dad? Isn't this . . . I thought I was calling Carters' Urban Rescue."

"You are. We're a family business."

"A family business that rescues wildlife? What will we think of next? Well . . . please relay this information to your father and see if he can do something for that poor, unfortunate deer. I really must dash. Good day, young lady."

Keisha heard the phone disconnect. She sat still for a minute, trying to figure out how a deer would get into the city in the first place. Then she remembered that Big Bob had once explained that deer could come into the city by traveling through "wildlife corridors," or stretches of nature that weren't proper forests. Wildlife corridors could be a city cemetery or urban garden, even a bunch of empty lots.

As Keisha flipped through the information they had on deer, she felt something cold and wet on her lap. The ice pack!

The lady on the phone wasn't the only one who would be late. Keisha still had to do her hair. Up the stairs, past the baby's room, where Mama sat in the rocking chair letting Paulo wake slowly by turning the beads on her necklace . . . Keisha called into her six-year-old brother Razi's room: "Your toad-in-the-hole is on the kitchen table!" She didn't wait for an answer. She kept running, past her own room with the ribbons displayed on her bed. She didn't know which one to put in her hair this morning. In fifth grade, it was so much more important to make the right choice.

"Grandma Alice?" Keisha knocked 'on the doorframe even though the door was open. "Sorry about cat-falling-off-counter. It looked good when you showed it to me yesterday."

"Mmmmmm." Grandma tried to roll over to face Keisha. "I don't think Grandma-falling-in-toilet-in-middle-of-night helped matters any," she said.

"Oh no. Did Razi forget to put the seat down again?"

"I would say so."

"I guess that means I should bring your toad-in-the-hole upstairs." Keisha started to leave but then stopped in the doorway. "I'm going to wear my purple hoodie," she told Grandma. "Ribbon color suggestions?"

"Ohhhhhh." Grandma shifted to lying on her back. She stared at the ceiling. "Are you feeling sassy, classy or Tallahassee?" Grandma felt your color choices should reflect your mood. A Tallahassee mood was very rare for Keisha. It was somewhere between bold and daring. Her friend Aaliyah was Tallahassee every other day. As for Keisha, she favored classy. But she didn't know her mood today. She was too busy running around.

"I'm not sure."

"Tie it up with butter yellow, and while you're at it, don't forget to butter the top of my toast."

Keisha started back down the hall. No matter how early she woke up, there was always something that kept her from getting ready in the morning in a leisurely fashion, the way Mama said getting ready should be done.

"Are you going to have science lab?" Grandma called out after Keisha had left the room.

Keisha's decision to turn back while rushing forward almost caused her to run into Mama and the baby.

"Yes."

"Well, wear the green, then. Marcus likes green."

"What is this? Wearing green for Marcus?" Mama handed Keisha baby Paulo, who was now busy sucking on a set of plastic keys.

Keisha buried her face in Paulo's soft, springy hair. *Grandma was so terrible at keeping secrets!*

"Why haven't I seen your brother this morning?" Mama wanted to know.

"He might be hiding."

Mama peered into Razi's room. She took the baby back. "You're the only one who can fit under there, Ada. Please get him to come out." Mama and Daddy called Keisha by her pet name, Ada, when they needed her to do something grown-up, like chase away one of Razi's bad moods. Ada meant "eldest daughter" in Igbo, the language Mama learned growing up in Nigeria.

Keisha didn't bother to turn on the light. She just slid under Razi's bed. He was pressed up against the far wall with his back to her.

"Razi-Roo?" Keisha whispered. "Daddy's making toad-in-the-hole for breakfast. We have to eat it now or we'll be late for school."

Razi gave a big snuffle but he didn't say anything. When Razi didn't say anything, it was a bad sign.

"Are you upset about Grandma?"

"Why did she yell at me?" He gulped, trying to swallow his tears. "I was fluffing her pillow like Mama does when we're sick!"

"She told me you forgot to put down the toilet seat."

"But *I* didn't forget." Razi was not trying to hide his crying now. Keisha put her hand on his back and pressed

just a little so he knew she was there to hear him.

"It's just like at school. All the other kids are talking, too, but Mrs. Jenkins says, 'Razi, do you need help to stop talking?' Angie's talking, Esteven's talking, Ronald's talking, but *I* have to go to the Peaceful Corner. I hate the Peaceful Corner."

It was a full-on cryorama, as Grandma would say, but Keisha could tell that Razi was coming to the end of it.

"Maybe if you have a good breakfast, you won't feel like talking," she said, tucking in the tails of Razi's shirt. "I'll think of something, Razi. Don't worry."

Razi rolled over and hugged his sister, smearing tears on top of baby Paulo's drool.

"Are the toads hiding?" he asked, sniffling just a

little. The toads were hiding when Daddy melted a piece of American cheese over the egg.

"Let's go find out." Keisha led Razi into the bathroom and wiped his face with a damp washcloth.

"Now, while I run into my bedroom a minute, I want you to look in that mirror and say, 'I, Razi Carter, am attracting the quiet energy of the universe to me.'" Grandma Alice taught the Carter children about affirmations and how you created your own good luck by thinking the right thoughts. While Razi looked in the mirror and repeated after Keisha, she ran into her bedroom and grabbed the pink ribbon off her bed. Pink and purple were royal and classy.

"Today will be a classy day," she told herself, just before tossing her springy curls over her head and pulling them together in a high ponytail. She dashed back to the bathroom, trying not to think about cold eggs.

"Let's go find some toads!" she told her brother with more enthusiasm than she felt. Toad-in-the-hole was Razi's favorite breakfast, not hers. She liked her eggs spread out, not all stacked up and jiggly, the way they got inside the toast hole.

Daddy must have read her mind because when they reached the kitchen, he pulled Razi's breakfast out of the oven and handed her something very different. "I saw you taking the phone call, so your first breakfast is now toad-in-Daddy's-stomach and I used some leftover potatoes to make you this. . . ."

Keisha took the plate. It had a fried egg on top of a nice big mound of hash browns.

"What's this?" Keisha asked, noting how thin and firm the white was—just how she liked it.

"I call it . . . uh . . . stingray-on-a-sandpile."

"It looks great. Thank you, Daddy." Keisha gave Daddy a big hug, which wasn't easy while holding a plate of stingray-on-a-sandpile.

"Better sit down and eat up, my girl. It's almost time to head to school."

Baby Paulo was smashing his breakfast with the back of his spoon, mashing everything together. Razi was eating his toast the Nigerian way, tearing it into strips and dipping it in his yolk. Not much food was finding its way into Razi's mouth, Keisha noticed.

"Keisha, have you looked in the mirror? It looks like your ponytail went south for the winter." Mama kissed the top of Keisha's head, exactly in the center, where ponytails belonged. "You can eat and have your hair done at the same time." Mama left the room and returned with an intake form in one hand and the round brush in the other.

Daddy sat down at the kitchen table with a pen. He pulled the intake form toward him. "We need a report about this call, so, given the extraordinary circum-stances, you are excused from the rule of not talking with your mouth full."

Keisha noticed that Razi didn't say what he usually said when Daddy excused Keisha from a rule—"That's not fair." He just sat there, dragging his toast through his yolk, then not eating it.

"She was rushing because she was late for work, so I didn't get all the normal information." Keisha was so hungry, she had to stop her report, pull off a strip of fried egg, roll some hash browns inside it, dip the whole business in her yolk and pop it into her mouth. Yum!

"I wrote her number down from the caller ID," Mama said, separating Keisha's hair from her elastic band.

"I remember her address," Keisha told Daddy. "422 Joan Street."

Daddy nibbled on the end of the pen. "That's not far away. Right by Huff Park."

"She was calling about a deer. She said it had a pumpkin stuck on its head."

Mama stopped brushing. "And how did this deer get a pumpkin stuck on its head?"

"She said she left the pumpkin outside with seeds in it as a treat for the birds."

"Let's examine the physics of this situation." Daddy

11

stood up and took a mixing bowl out of the cupboard. "So I'm a deer and I see a pumpkin with some nice fresh seeds inside it. Yum, yum." With his head in the bowl, Daddy made smacking noises. "Uh-oh, it's stuck. Whoa!" Daddy started lumbering around the kitchen, bumping into the counter and the table. "Who turned the lights out?"

Watching Daddy made baby Paulo giggle. His

jiggling tummy made the high-chair tray vibrate. Razi looked up from his plate. He started to giggle, too.

"Wait a minute!" Keisha said. "The deer could see." She started to put another bite of food in her mouth but then held it there, remembering. "I know because the lady said it was going down the trail that led to the baseball diamonds. And you can't take a trail if you can't see. Right?"

"Well, then." Daddy took the bowl off his head and dropped into his chair. "This is a wildlife mystery."

"The other question," Mama pondered as she snapped the elastic band in place, "is how does a pumpkin get stuck on a deer's head? Pumpkins are heavy and slick inside."

"Seems like he could just smack it against a tree and break it up," Daddy said.

"Can we go to the park after school and look for the deer, Daddy? I don't have jump rope practice today." Keisha had won a place on the Grand River Steppers Jump Rope Team, but they didn't have practice on Tuesdays.

"Let's hope your daddy finds the poor deer before then," Mama said. "Who knows how long he's had this problem. I'm worried he'll get dehydrated. Besides, we're making your costume today." Mama had found an old sheet that she thought had enough snowy white parts to make the apron and the head cover that Phillis Wheatley, the first published African American poet, wore. As a costume, it wasn't very exciting. What Keisha really wanted to be for Halloween was a Romany girl. Ever since Grandma told her about the Romany people and how much they loved their dogs, well . . . But Mr. Drockmore, their fifth-grade teacher, was giving extra credit to students who dressed up to give their oral reports in social studies.

Mama curled a piece of Keisha's hair around her finger. "But let's take care of after school *after* school. Now is the time to run up and brush your teeth and . . . go get the green ribbon."

Keisha turned around and looked up at her mother.

"What? Regardless of what your grandma says, it is the best color for your purple hoodie."

Chapter 2

As they put on their coats, Keisha remembered her promise to help Razi stay quiet during the school day. Razi's first-grade teacher, Mrs. Jenkins, didn't allow children to bring things from home that might provide a distraction, but she sometimes made an exception for the super-squeezy concentration ball. It was a ball Big Bob had given Grandma to keep her fingers strong, but the Carters found that it helped Razi remember to stay quiet if he squeezed it whenever he felt like talking. Mama kept the super-squeezy concentration ball in a basket in the hall, along with the hats and mittens the children used when it got cold. It was such a warm fall, the children didn't need their hats and mittens yet, so Keisha had to dig around for it. She stuck it in her pocket when Razi wasn't looking.

The fresh air seemed to give her brother new energy. He bounded down the front steps, picked up a stick and ran ahead of Keisha. As he ran, he made up a song to go along with the rhythm of the stick he was dragging across every chain-link fence they passed.

"Razi!" Keisha called after him. When the chain-link fence by the Tuttles' house ended, the Bakers' wooden fence began. Keisha knew that behind the wooden fence sat Harvey the dog, just waiting for someone to bark at.

Keisha blamed Harvey for making Razi say that if the Carter family ever got a household pet, he wanted a kitty, *not* a puppy. So far, Mama said no domestic pets. That meant no animals that lived inside. The Carters had enough animals to care for without adding a pet, thank you very much, and everyone who lived in the house had to pull their own weight. Except for the baby.

But ever since Keisha had read Beverly Cleary's *Henry and Ribsy*, and *101 Dalmatians* and *Lassie Come-Home*, she was convinced that if you wanted to have adventures, it was much more likely with a dog. That was why she decided to be a Romany girl before she learned about the extra credit in Mr. Drockmore's class. The Romany people had dogs all over the place, for protecting and hunting, and maybe for waiting at home by the caravan, with their adorable tongues hanging out and their behinds wiggling.

Sure enough, as soon as Harvey heard the stick dragging along the wooden fence, he started running on the other side, barking his loud, growly bark and making a ruckus of his own.

"Wait for me, Razi!"

But Razi was famous for ignoring his sister when he got scared. He started to run even faster. Would he remember to look both ways if he got to the end of the block first?

Fortunately, Mr. Sanders, their postman, was coming down the street from the opposite direction. He stuck out his arms and said, "In the name of the United States Postal Service, I order you to halt, young man."

Razi leapt into Mr. Sanders's arms, which was not

easy for Mr. Sanders because his arms were already full of mail.

"After that display of athleticism, I'm going to guess you are a track star for Halloween this year."

"I'm not going to be a track star," Razi said, breathing hard. "I'm going to be a police officer and give that dog a bad-doggy ticket."

Keisha caught up. "No he's not. He's going to be an alligator. Mama made the costume this summer."

"And what are you going to be, Miss Keisha?"

"Well, I was going to be a Romany girl, but I'm not sure because—"

"You will excuse my ignorance, but what is a Romany girl?"

"Grandma told me that I love dogs so much, I should be a Romany girl. They used to be called Gypsies because people thought they were from Egypt. But they really came from India."

"That's fascinating, Keisha. I think you should be a Romany girl, too."

"For Romany people, dogs weren't just pets. They were necessary. Romany dogs definitely pulled their own weight."

"I'm going to be a police officer and make Harvey sit in the Peaceful Corner. He talks more than I do."

Mr. Sanders put Razi back on his own two feet. "Why do I feel so confused this morning? Did I miss something?" he said.

"Oh, Razi, you're an alligator. And I wasn't finished." Keisha turned back to Mr. Sanders. "I'm not exactly sure yet because Mr. Drockmore said he'd give extra credit to students who delivered their reports in costume. My report is on the first published African American poet, Phillis Wheatley."

Mr. Sanders scooped up a few advertising leaflets he'd dropped on the ground. "That's right. Zeke and Zack were trying to decide whether to be George Washington and John Adams or a hamburger and fries."

"What are you going to be, Mr. Sanders?" Like Daddy, Keisha knew Mr. Sanders always dressed up.

"It's a secret," Mr. Sanders said.

"Tell me. Tell me! I can keep a secret," Razi said.

Mr. Sanders ruffled Razi's hair. "I know you can. But it's such a big secret, I haven't told it to myself yet."

"That doesn't make any sense," Razi declared.

Keisha covered her mouth so Razi wouldn't hear her giggle.

"What I *don't* want to be is late on my delivery route. Or to make either of you late for school. So I think we'd better scoot."

"Bye, Mr. Sanders." Keisha took her brother's hand and they set off again.

Even though Razi kept looking back and begging Keisha to let him run and ask if Mr. Sanders was delivering any packages for him, they managed to make it to school on time.

"And how is our Razi this morning?" Mrs. Jenkins hugged Razi as soon as he reached the first-grade line. Razi tucked his chin farther inside his shirt. She had on a wool blazer and Razi didn't like the way wool felt. It was too scratchy.

"Very well, thank you," Razi mumbled, staring at the ground.

Keisha could tell that seeing Mrs. Jenkins reminded Razi of his problems at school.

Mrs. Jenkins untucked Razi's chin and cupped it in her hand. She leaned back so she could look into his eyes. "We're going to decorate our treat bags today, and I need someone to demonstrate making pumpkin faces. But he must be cheerful."

"Oh! Oh!" Razi waved his hand so wildly, he bonked Keisha on the head.

"Mrs. Jenkins?" Keisha slipped the ball out of her pocket and passed it to her.

Razi was so busy trying to be chosen, he didn't notice.

"Just in case," Keisha said.

"You'd best line up, dear." Mrs. Jenkins put the ball into her coat pocket. "I see the fifth graders going to their classrooms."

Keisha kissed her brother on the top of his head before running across the playground. As long as you were in line when your class went through the big glass doors, you were not considered late. Keisha caught up to Zeke and Zack just before they went into the building.

"You're always here before us," Zeke said.

"No she's not," Zack argued.

"Yes she is."

"No. Yesterday she wasn't."

Keisha put one hand on each of their shoulders. At least something was going the way it was supposed to this morning. Daddy called Zeke and Zack the Z-Team. They were nice to everybody else, but they almost always disagreed with each other.

"I was just talking to your dad. Hamburger and fries? I thought you were for sure about Washington and Adams."

"It depends on how we did on our social studies quiz. Mom is hoping for the food because that would be easier to make."

"She likes construction more than sewing."

"And fast food more than cooking."

The Sanderses lived a few houses down on Horton Street, so the boys came over a lot while Mrs. Sanders attended classes at Grand River Community College to get her associate's degree in botany. The Z-Team liked to check in after school to see what smells were coming from Mama's kitchen.

As soon as Mr. Drockmore took attendance, Keisha did her morning freewriting about Harvey the barking menace and how his bad behavior would make sure she never got a puppy . . . ever! Now if Mama let them have a pet, they would have to get a hamster or, at best, a kitten. But you couldn't take a kitten to obedience class, could you? Kittens didn't stand by the door with tails thumping, waiting for you to come home and take them out for an adventure. Maybe they wouldn't get any pet at all.

After freewriting came math, and after math, the students worked on science observations. One of the things Keisha liked most about Mr. Drockmore was that he sometimes let students choose their own project teams. Aaliyah, Jorge, Marcus and Wen were Keisha's friends *and* her science project team. Today they were studying the density of water at different temperatures. Yesterday they had frozen colored-water ice cubes.

Today they were watching what happened when they dropped the ice cubes in a jar of hot water.

"Oooh. It looks like a red jellyfish." Aaliyah pointed to the melting ice cube. Little tentacles of color were coming out of the bottom. "Speaking of red . . . does anybody know where I can get a piece of red carpet?"

"It's getting less dense as it melts," Wen said as she wrote in their observation notebook.

"What do you want a red carpet for?" Marcus had his head down. He was drawing a jellyfish on a piece of copy paper. Later they would paste it in their science notebook. Marcus had earned them a lot of extra credit points that way.

"I'm going to be a red-carpet celebrity for Halloween."

"For real?" Marcus stopped drawing and looked up at Aaliyah. "Which one?"

"I thought you were going to be Sojourner Truth," Wen said.

"I *could* use the extra points . . . but have you seen the way that woman dressed? She'll ruin my reputation in the neighborhoods!" Even though Aaliyah lived in the Garfield Park neighborhood, she thought of Alger Heights, where Keisha lived, as her home, too, since her grandma—whom all the kids called Moms—lived in Alger Heights and Aaliyah went to Moms's house most days after school.

"There's a sign outside Verhey Carpet saying that they sell squares for fifty cents," Wen informed Aaliyah.

"You could be Sojourner Truth at school and Beyoncé when you trick-or-treat," Marcus pointed out.

"Marcus, a fourth-to-fifth cannot be seen in the Halloween line dance with an old-lady shawl and a funny hat. I have a reputation to protect. Besides, Alicia Keys is my girl. Beyoncé is too la-di-da."

"I know what you mean." Wen closed the notebook. "Abigail Adams wore the same funny outfit."

"I think school should be school and Halloween Halloween," Marcus said. "Maybe we should have a revolution."

The Fantastic Fifth Graders, or FFGs, as Mr. Drockmore called them, had begun the year studying American history. The unit finished right around Halloween, so everyone in class knew a lot about the American Revolution and the period leading up to the Civil War.

"But it's a tradition," Wen said.

"Well, isn't that what revolutions are for?" Marcus asked. "Making a change?"

Social studies was in the afternoon, after lunch. With only a few days to go before their presentations on

Friday, students were busy making the posters they would use to give their oral reports. Mr. Drockmore had let them draw numbers to choose their famous person. Keisha had drawn number six, and she got her first choice. She loved learning about Phillis Wheatley because Keisha liked to write, too, and Phillis had this great flowy handwriting that was fun to copy. Though it was amazing that Phillis could be brought to America as a slave and learn English like a native speaker in less than a year and a half, Keisha didn't really get her poetry. Grandma called it "highfalutin."

The classroom was quiet while they created, except for the squeak of markers and the sound of cutting construction paper. Mr. Drockmore was busy at his desk, filling in his planner.

"Mr. Drockmore." Marcus stood up as if he was going to make a speech. Everyone turned to look at him. Mr. Drockmore closed his planner.

"Mr. Pearce."

"Permission to address the assembly."

"Permission granted."

Zeke and Zack scooted their chairs closer to Marcus, who held up a piece of paper and read: "We the people of the fifth grade of Langston Hughes Elementary, in order to form a more perfect Halloween, establish new

traditions, ensure a good time, provide for FFG creativity, remain consistent with other grades' costumes and secure the blessings of future generations, do request to establish that we can wear our favorite costumes on Halloween and give our oral reports in them, so that we can rock the line dance, have more fun and only make one costume."

Wen and Keisha looked at each other with a wide-open-eyed giggle. Would it work?

Mr. Drockmore clapped his hands. "That's a very nice play on the words of the Constitution, Marcus."

"We helped him during lunch," Zeke said.

Zack raised his hand. "Yeah, we thought about staging a revolution, but then we decided to ask first."

"What I don't understand"—Mr. Drockmore twisted the cap on his whiteboard marker—"is why you don't like the idea. Last year's Fantastic Fifth Graders seemed to really enjoy this assignment."

"We're different," Zeke added. "We like science better."

Mr. Drockmore smiled. "And what does science have to do with not dressing up as your famous person?"

"Engineering is science, isn't it?" Zack asked. "Our mom said she's going to have to turn into a construction engineer if we have enough social studies points."

"And why is that?" Mr. Drockmore asked.

"We really want to be a hamburger and French fries."

Now Wen raised her hand. "Creating your own costume exercises your creativity. And you have always told us that scientists have to be good at imagining things that don't exist yet."

Keisha raised one hand and, with the other, pointed to the back of the room, to Mr. Drockmore's poster of his hero, Albert Einstein. "Mr. Einstein did say imagination was more important than knowledge."

"Whoa! Whoa!" Mr. Drockmore held up his hands.

"You're triple-, quadruple-teaming me. Time-out. I'll discuss this with you individually when you give me your progress reports. Then I'll make a decision." Mr. Drockmore opened his planning book again, signaling that it was time for the class to get back to their independent work. "I must say . . . you are a determined bunch of patriots."

During afternoon recess, as Wen, Aaliyah and Keisha sat on one of the benches waiting for their turn to jump, Keisha told them all about Phillis Wheatley.

"During my conference, Mr. Drockmore said it was a great idea to recite one of her poems," Keisha told the girls.

"Did you pick yet?" Aaliyah asked. "Practice on us."

Keisha bit her lip. "Okay. 'Ode to Neptune' . . . um . . . 'While raging tempests shake the shore, while Aeolus' thunders round us roar, and sweep im—' um, 'impet—' "

"Impetuous?" Wen had listened to Keisha recite the day before at jump rope practice.

" 'Impetuous over the plain . . . be still, O tyrant of the main.' "

Ms. Tellerico, the principal, blew the whistle for first-half recess. The girls stood up and brushed off their bottoms.

"Our turn. I'm jumpin' first," Aaliyah said.

Keisha and Wen took the rope from Therese and Erica. Aaliyah was jumping before they even started to swing the ropes. "This is how you remember your report, Key. Look at me! Look at me! I plow and I plant and I chop down trees. Look at me! I'm so strong. I can jump rope all night long." Aaliyah jumped out and took the rope from Keisha.

"That's not exactly how her speech goes," Wen said.

"I'm giving Sojourner Truth a makeover."

"I think you should be Serena or Venus Williams for Halloween," Keisha said. "Not a red-carpet celebrity. If Sojourner Truth were alive now, she'd be an athlete."

"You could wear one of your mom's tennis dresses," Wen suggested.

"I do look good in white," Aaliyah said. "And I'm almost as tall as my mom, *and* I could run between houses faster. Hmmm . . ."

Since the fourth-to-fifth wing had the last lunchtime of the day, the afternoon always went by more quickly than the morning. Just before the bell rang for the walkers, Mr. Drockmore told the class that he would review their comments *and* their social studies quiz grades and let them know his decision about the costumes tomorrow. Keisha tugged her backpack out of her locker and lined up. Mr. Drockmore always excused the family elders first so they could go get their brothers and sisters before things got crazy. She ran across the playground to the K–1 wing, reaching it just as the children were lining up to march outside.

Mrs. Jenkins stood with the super-squeezy concentration ball held out in front of her. Razi was in line, pinching his lips together with his fingers. Uh-oh.

"The ball helped at first," Mrs. Jenkins told Keisha when she got close. "Razi had a good morning, and I told him I was confident that he could have a Peaceful Corner–free day today. But during library time with Ms. Fontarelli, the ball got away from him three times. The last time, it rolled under the Dr. Seuss fish tank and, after retrieving it, he emerged covered in dust bunnies with a poor, dehydrated dead blue fish in his hand."

Mrs. Jenkins paused to button up her blazer. "At that point, Razi exercised poor judgment, choosing to wave the fish in front of the three children he knew would scream the loudest. To top it off, he declared that he would bring the fish back to life with the abracadabra stick, and he went into Ms. Fontarelli's desk without permission."

Keisha put the super-squeezy concentration ball into her pocket. She noticed that Mrs. Jenkins had buttoned her blazer up wrong, putting the top button into the second buttonhole. Should she say something to Mrs. Jenkins about that?

Mrs. Jenkins raised her hand so that all walkers knew to keep their mouths closed and their hands to themselves while walking outside. Keisha walked alongside the group. She then waited until Mrs. Jenkins released the walkers, grabbed the Razi hand that wasn't pinching his lips and pulled her brother along toward home.

When they got in sight of the house, Razi broke away and rushed up the back stairs into the warm kitchen, where Mama, Daddy and Big Bob were sitting at the table with slices of ginger cake and cups of coffee. By the time Keisha got into the kitchen, his face was buried in Mama's skirt.

"What is this?" Mama asked, rubbing circles into Razi's back as he cried. "Did we spend more time in the Peaceful Corner today?"

"I wonder why they call it the Peaceful Corner." Daddy put his hand on Mama's. "Our little Razi-Roo never feels very peaceful when he's in it."

While Mama fed Razi bits of ginger cake and listened to the story of his day, Keisha cut her own slice and went to sit between Daddy and Big Bob.

Grandma always said when you were having a not-so-Tallahassee day, you had to be on the lookout for good things to balance you out. Good things seemed to hover around Big Bob.

"I know just how you feel, buddy. Remind me sometime to tell you about my finger-painting disaster of 1946. Want to sit on my shoes?" Big Bob asked Razi after Mama rubbed his teary face with her napkin. Big Bob was so big that you could sit on his shoes and lean back, and it was the perfect place for Razi to play under the table with the nuts and bolts in the Carter family toolbox.

After Razi was settled, the conversation continued. They were talking about Big Bob's recent visit to his sister's house.

"Anyway . . ." Big Bob took another sip of coffee. "It was so good to see Betty. She found a box of my mother's jewelry, and she wanted each of us to pick out something to keep. As you can imagine, I didn't have the faintest idea. But I thought our Alice might like this." Big Bob reached into his shirt pocket and pulled out a ring. It looked tiny in his palm. He passed it to Mama, who held it up to the light. The Carters oohed as it flashed green sparkles all across the room.

Razi's head popped up from underneath the table. "Can I see it? Please! Please, Big Bob. I can be careful."

"Of course you can," Big Bob said. He caught Razi's waving hand and examined the fingers. "I think it will fit your thumb. Then you can look at yourself in the mirror and be the king of Horton Street."

Mama passed the ring back, and Razi stood very still while Big Bob put the ring on his thumb.

Everyone turned to watch Razi scamper down the hall. Mama said, "It is a lovely ring, Bob, though I'm not sure it will fit Alice. Is it an emerald?"

Big Bob nodded. "Emerald was my mom's birthstone. According to Betty, it was Mom's favorite ring. I thought if Alice liked it . . . well, that would be a way to honor Mom. I know she would have loved Alice, but of course Mom was long gone by the time I met—" Bob stopped talking and stared at the tops of his hands. "Maybe Alice could wear it on her pinky. That's fashion-forward, isn't it, Keisha? A pinky ring?"

Big Bob looked at Keisha as if she would know such a thing. "I'll ask Aaliyah," she said. "She has a subscription to *Stylin' Teen*."

Razi ran back into the room, waving his arm. "I am the king of all that I see," he declared. "But now it is time to fix my drawbridge." He pulled the ring off his thumb and handed it back to Big Bob. Then he disappeared under the table.

"Didn't you say on the phone there was something

else you wanted to talk about?" Daddy asked Big Bob. "Something about a pup?"

Keisha glanced at Mama. Could it be? Had they told Big Bob to be on the lookout for a puppy?

But Mama just looked curious.

"Oh, right. We got a pup at the Humane Society and he's causing quite a commotion. Dr. Wendy thought you might be able to help."

"With all those dogs, how does one puppy cause a commotion?" Mama asked.

"Well . . ." Big Bob paused. He looked as if he didn't know how to begin. "I was there when they brought him in. Poor thing seemed scared of his own shadow. I just spent a little time petting him, trying to calm him down. It seems he took a liking to me, and now . . . whenever I show up, he sets to howling."

"Sure you don't have a wolf pup there?" Daddy asked. "Same animal family."

"No. Dr. Wendy said it's not a wolf pup. But it might be coyote. Or a cross."

"A coydog? Where did they find him?" Mama asked.

"A farmer found him out in his field. In Allegan. He thought about keeping him, but his other dogs wouldn't have him. They kept deviling the poor little guy." Big Bob had been turning the ring in his fingers. Now he put it in his pocket. "We're not sure what to do with him. That howling means he's more than a mutt. He's got a good bit, if not a whole bunch, of wild in him. I was wondering if you'd take a look, Fred."

"No!" Razi's head popped out from under the table. "Right, Mama? No dogs allowed!"

"Razi Carter." Mama's voice was firm as she leaned down to speak to him under the table. "You do not make the decisions in this family. Bob and Dr. Wendy are asking for our help. When we ask for their help, Bob and Dr. Wendy help us. As my father used to say, 'One hand cannot clean itself.'" Mama straightened and said to Big Bob: "Your puppy can stay with us a few days in a pen in the back, Bob." She gave Keisha a serious look before adding, "If it is wild, it belongs here."

"Did the farmer give him a name?" Keisha asked. "When he thought he would keep him?"

"Nonononono," Razi was saying under the table. "No dogs allowed. I said no! Bad dog, Harvey."

"Don't interrupt, Razi," Daddy said.

"Racket," Bob said, raising his voice so he could be heard.

"Racket?"

"That's how the farmer found him. Sitting at the

side of the field, just a-hollerin' his poor little head off and making a racket."

"Ada," Mama whispered. "Run tell Grandma she has a visitor."

"Doggies are bad. Bad dog, Harvey!"

"Razi Carter! Don't make me tell you again." Mama was using her stern voice.

As she bounded up the stairs, Keisha thought that even though Razi didn't like dogs, he and this puppy had at least one thing in common—racket making.

Chapter 3

Just as Keisha was returning to the kitchen, Zeke and Zack knocked on the back door and called out, "Hello, hello! Anyone home?" The Z-Team were like family to the Carters, so the boys opened the door without anyone having to get up.

"Any ginger cake left?" Zeke asked. "Mom is drying leaves in the microwave for her collection, and she says if you have some ginger cake to feed us now, she'll take us all to identify bark later."

"I have an extra one warming in the oven." Mama reached for the hot pads. "I talked to your mama this afternoon."

"I'm afraid Keisha can't go." Daddy helped himself to another slice. "I'll just finish up this cold cake so we can set the pan to soak."

"What?" Zack wasn't happy about this. "Keisha's the one who pays attention."

It was true that Keisha had more patience for Mrs. Sanders's biology lectures than Zeke or Zack. Maybe that was because she had a lot of practice listening to Daddy talk about animals.

Zack took Grandma's chair, and Zeke sat in the chair that Big Bob had just left on his way to visit with Grandma.

"You can lean on my legs if you want, Razi," Zeke told him, stretching his legs out as far as they would go. "How come you can't go with us, Keisha?"

Mama served Zack and Zeke two big slices of cake. Keisha took Big Bob's plate and the cake pan to the sink, filled it with soapy water, and started to wash the dishes, waiting for Daddy to explain. Sometimes he didn't want everyone to know about their business. And if the Z-Team told their dad, a lot of people on his route would know by the end of delivery time tomorrow.

"Well, boys . . ." Daddy stretched out after his snack, clasping his hands behind his head. "The truth is, we have work to do. We got a D.I.D. report this morning and we need to go check it out."

"You got a 'did'?"

"Yup. Over at Huff Park."

"That's way better than looking at bark," Zack said, even though his mouth was full. "Can we come with you?"

Keisha knew for a fact that the Z-Team did not know what a D.I.D. was because she didn't know what a D.I.D. was. *Deer in Darkness? Deer in Danger?*

"If it's nature, Mom will let us go. Please!"

"Yeah. It gets so boring when she goes into her tree trance."

"What's a tree trance?" Razi wanted to know.

"That's when she stops moving and looks at the tree for a long time," Zeke said, and he let his mouth drop open like he was stupefied.

"She doesn't like us to talk while she's doing it, either," Zack told them. "*Or* find sticks for a fort."

"And what, Mr. Carter, is a D.I.D.?" Mama asked, pulling the pitcher of milk out of the refrigerator.

"I'm surprised you don't remember, Mrs. Carter. 'D.I.D.' stands for 'Deer in Distress.' "

More than a few crumbs escaped Zack's wide-open mouth. "Deer in Distress?"

"I never saw a deer up close," Zeke said. "Just on TV. Can we come? Please?!"

"Well, I can call your mom, but I can't promise we'll see the deer," Daddy told the boys. "I tried to track it this morning, but no luck."

"Yes you will find it." Razi's voice rose from underneath the table. "Because he has a pumpkin on his head. And Grandma says wearing the color orange always gets you noticed."

"A what?"

"How?" Zeke and Zack were filled with questions.

Keisha and Daddy answered them as best they could.

"So we're just going to check it out," Daddy said. "And we'll try to track the deer, but there's no guarantee we'll find it."

"We can ride our bikes," Zeke said.

"Deal," Daddy said. "I'll bring the truck, just in case we need it. We'll park at the end of Joan Street and walk down from there. While you boys go home and get your bikes *and* permission, we can see if the lady who reported the deer is back from work. Razi-Roo?" Daddy bent his long body over and stuck his head under the table. "Will you come and help us find the deer?"

"Can I do somersaults?" Razi asked.

"As many as you like."

Razi climbed out from under the table. Mama pulled him toward her for a cuddle. "I'll stay here and feed the little bunnies," Mama said.

A construction worker had found a den of baby bunnies on a site about to be leveled, and the Carters were helping to fatten them up so they could survive the coming winter in the wild. Mama added, "And I'll get out a crate for our new visitor. *And* I'll work on my soup because Mr. Sanders is sure to stop by after his route."

Since Mrs. Sanders used her kitchen for biology experiments more than cooking, Mr. Sanders was also a common guest at the Carters' house.

"Wait a minute. You're getting a new animal?" Zeke pressed his finger on all the crumbs on his plate and licked them up. "What is it?"

"I bet it's a bear," Zack said.

"Maybe it's another alligator," Zeke added, remembering their adventure with an alligator in the city pool last summer.

"Can we see it? Pleeeeeease?"

Mama laughed. "You can't see what isn't here yet. Run home and get your bikes. Maybe a little riding will help you work off all that noisy energy. Tracking a deer is quiet work."

Keisha put her hands on her brother's shoulders and chug-chugged him out the door to the truck. Even though she was big enough to ride up front, Keisha sat in the backseat with Razi. "Want to play rock, paper, scissors?" she asked her brother.

"No, but thank you very much for inquiring." Razi stared out the window.

Daddy's glance met Keisha's in the rearview mirror. Razi loved rock, paper, scissors.

"We'll track that deer, but I think we're going to have to track your smile, too, Razi," Daddy said.

It was a short ride. They parked at the end of Joan Street, on a bare stretch of ground next to a sign with a picture of a hiker. An arrow pointed between the houses and down the hill into the park.

"There's 422 Joan Street, Daddy." Keisha jumped out of the truck and rang the doorbell. By the time Daddy and Razi caught up, she had already figured out there was no one at home.

"Hmmm," Daddy said. "I thought she might still be at work. I didn't want to go on her property this morning, but I wonder if she'd mind if we took a look out back now. We might find a print."

Keisha tugged on Daddy's shirt. A man had come out of the garage next door, carrying a rake.

"Excuse me." Daddy stepped off the porch and walked over to the neighbor's yard. "We're from Carters' Urban Rescue. I'm Fred Carter and these are my children, Keisha and Razi. We got a call this morning about a deer with a pumpkin on its head, and we've come over to investigate. But no one's home. Do you think your neighbor would mind if we went into her backyard to check for tracks?"

The man stuck out his hand. "Dan Gorman. Pleased to meet you. Go on and check out the backyard. I'm sure Prissy wouldn't mind." Mr. Gorman scratched his belly and leaned on his rake. "But that deer is long gone."

"Does she have any bad doggies back there?" Razi peeked out from behind Daddy; his finger was curled in Daddy's belt loop.

"Nope. Just a cat that sits in the window."

"Does the cat have soft fur?" Razi asked.

"Standard-issue," Mr. Gorman replied.

Keisha did not want to get into a conversation that covered all the wonderful things about cats. "Pleased to meet you," she said, holding out her hand the way Daddy had taught her and looking the man straight in the eye.

"That's a nice handshake, young lady."

"Did you see the deer, too, Mr. Gorman?"

"I should say so. Didn't have my glasses on at the time. Looked like a pumpkin was bobbing along in the air. We see more deer here than you'd think, being in the city and all."

"So it really did have a pumpkin on its head. . . ." Daddy crossed his arms and looked at the sky, the way he did when he was thinking things over.

"My grandbaby girl is in the hospital getting her tonsils out, and I thought it would cheer her up some if I took a picture of it. But now I can't find the picture!"

"You lost your camera?"

"No. It's on this newfangled contraption." Mr. Gorman pulled a cell phone out of his pocket and held it out to Daddy. "Maybe you know something about these things."

"Not much, I'm afraid, except to make and take phone calls. But I bet our Razi here can find it." Daddy waited for Mr. Gorman to nod his approval before he handed the cell phone to Razi.

"Give it a try, young fella. It was a birthday present from my girls, and Tracyanne tells me there's nothing I can do to break it except for dropping it in the Grand River. The buttons are so little, I can barely see 'em. That's what getting old does for you."

Razi cupped the cell phone in both his hands. Keisha had seen him do this before with handheld games, TV remotes, even Mr. Sanders's new digital camera. He could barely read, but Grandma said that Razi intuited the way things worked.

They all watched as Razi started pressing buttons. After a few distressing bleeps from the phone, an image of a camera popped up. "Here it is!"

"Good job, Razi." Daddy held out his hand. "Can I see?"

"Wait a minute. . . ." Razi's nose touched the keypad as he pulled the phone close. "That's *my* pumpkin!"

"It can't be your pumpkin," Daddy said. "I just stepped over Jack-o'-Lantern in the front hall."

"No! The one I use for trick-or-treating."

"That's a plastic pumpkin, Razi. Give me the phone, please." Keisha was about to grab it from her brother when Zeke and Zack rode up on their bikes.

"Hey there!" Zack dropped his bike on the ground while Zeke leaned his against Mr. Gorman's garage.

"Well, hello," Mr. Gorman said. "Are you part of the rescue squad, too?"

"We're here about a deer in distress," Zeke said, out of breath.

"Can I see, too?" Zack asked, reaching for the phone. He and Keisha bumped heads as Razi held it out.

"Maybe we should agree to pass the phone around to avoid on-the-job injuries. As the elder, I will go first." Daddy took the phone and squinted at the image on the screen. "Well, now I've seen everything." He gave the phone to Keisha.

Razi was hopping up and down. "We have to get my pumpkin back. It's almost Halloween!"

"And what are you going to be for Halloween?" Mr. Gorman asked. "Tracyanne junior is going to be a pirate."

"I'm going to be a police officer."

"No you're not. You're going to be an alligator," Zeke said. "Keisha, quit hogging."

"Hold your horses, mister." Keisha wasn't ready to let go yet. The photograph was too small to see well, but it looked like a young deer was snooping inside a plastic pumpkin, looking for food, or maybe even water. But the part that didn't make sense was that the pumpkin was off the ground. Somehow it was stuck to the deer's head.

Zack put his chin on Keisha's shoulder. "How come he doesn't just pull his nose out?"

"Don't say *his* nose," Zeke said to his brother. "Boy deer have antlers. This is a girl deer."

"Right. Girls are always sticking their noses where they don't belong."

Keisha was about to defend the girls of the world when Daddy asked her, "Can you send that photo to our computer at home? That way, we can blow it up and get a closer look."

Razi grabbed the cell phone out of Keisha's hands and started punching buttons.

"Careful, Razi," Daddy cautioned. Then he pointed down the slope to an opening in the woods below. "Is that the trail that leads to the ball diamonds?"

"It is, but first you have to go through the wetland area."

"Hmmm." Daddy rubbed his chin.

"There." Razi handed the phone back to Mr. Gorman. "I just sent it to everybody," he said.

"But what about Daddy? He's not in Mr. Gorman's address book. Can I see it for a minute, Mr. Gorman?"

"Be my guest," Mr. Gorman replied.

"Can I be your guest, too?" Razi tugged on Mr. Gorman's sleeve. "Do you have cookies?"

Mr. Gorman nodded. "I must warn you, though. I'm a bachelor. They're cookies from a package."

Cell phones weren't hard to figure out. Soon Keisha had sent the photo to their home e-mail.

Daddy shook Mr. Gorman's hand. "We'll take a rain check on the cookies. Thank you kindly for your assistance. And if we find this deer, you'll be the first to know."

"With trackers like these, I think you have a good chance."

Keisha looked at Zack and Zeke and Razi, who were busy chest-bumping each other. Then she looked up at Mr. Gorman. Was he serious?

Chapter 4

"Let's take a walk, kids, and see if we can spot some tracks. By the way, boys, I wouldn't be so certain that this is a girl deer. It might be a button buck that—"

"We're on the hill now, Daddy," Razi broke in. "Can I somersault down there?"

Daddy nodded and Keisha watched Razi run down the hill, his arms flung out to catch the breeze. He looked happy for the first time all afternoon.

"What's a button buck?" Zeke wanted to know.

"Well, in their first year of life, male deer don't grow a full set of antlers. They just have what are called horn buds."

"I didn't see any buds," Zack said. "I still think it's a girl. Wait for me, Razi!"

Zeke and Zack ran after Razi.

"I can do four in a row," Razi bragged.

"We can do more than that!"

"So what did you make of that little picture, Key?" Daddy asked. "The screen was too small for me to see. We'll blow it up when we get home and be able to tell whether we say 'he' or 'she.' "

"It doesn't really matter, does it?" Keisha asked. "It's in trouble, either way. Somehow that pumpkin is stuck tight."

The boys raced over the wooden boardwalk that crossed the marsh. As they got closer, Keisha heard a gurgling stream.

Daddy stepped off the trail and squatted down. "With the rain recently, I thought maybe . . ."

Keisha squatted next to him.

"Here, little deer!" Razi called out from a distance. "Come here and I'll pull the pumpkin off your head!"

"Shhhhh!" said Zack or Zeke. "You're scaring him away, Razi."

"I'll give you a cookie. . . ."

"Here we go." Daddy was pointing to a set of tracks. It was easy to spot deer tracks. Unlike squirrels or chipmunks, or other animals you might see in the park, deer had hooves. Their tracks looked a little like bunny ears, with the tops close together but not touching.

"These are full-sized tracks," Daddy said. "I don't think they belong to a button buck or a fawn born this spring." He stood up, keeping his eyes on the ground.

Keisha followed him, examining the leaves and branches. "Look, Daddy." She pointed to a stand of bushes growing along the stream bank. The bushes had bite marks down low and high up.

Daddy grabbed one of the low branches. "Hmmm. And look down here."

Keisha followed Daddy's finger and saw another set of hoofprints, only these were much smaller. "Mamas and babies stay together for about a year," Daddy said. "I wonder what Mama thought when her baby deer came home with a pumpkin on its head."

Before Keisha could answer, she and Daddy were interrupted by a crashing and snapping of twigs. It was Zack. "Ummm, we need some help with Razi. He's up a tree again."

"That would be a B. I. D." Daddy dropped his nibbled twig. They followed Zack back to the boardwalk and down the path until they came to an old oak tree.

"I was watching him, honest!" Zeke said. "I just stopped to tie my shoe."

"I was trying to catch a frog," Zack confessed.

Nobody had to tell Keisha what happened. Mama always said Razi was part monkey. When he found a tree to climb with a good branch low enough to swing up, he couldn't resist.

"I can see the deer!" Razi called to them from the branches. The fall had been so warm that the trees hadn't shed as many of their leaves as usual. It was hard to see exactly how far up Razi was.

Daddy cupped his hands around his mouth and called up, "It doesn't really matter if you can see the deer, Razi-Roo, because we can't see you. And seeing you is the first order of business."

"I am the king of all that I see!" Razi shouted. "Key, come up here with me."

Keisha had already pulled herself up onto the first branch. Razi was like a baby bear. He liked to go up, but he didn't always know how to get down. Looking down and seeing how high up he was frightened Razi. This wasn't the first time Keisha had to talk him down from a tree.

"I want to see the deer, too, Razi. Can I join you?"

"I command you to make me a ladder," Razi ordered Keisha once she'd touched his shoe to let him know she was close.

"One ladder for King Razi." She squeezed Razi's left foot. "Put this one on it first," she said. "Hold on with your hands and I'll show you."

"I can see Horton Street! There's Mama and baby Paulo!"

They were not high up enough to see Horton Street, but with Keisha nearby, Razi could enjoy being up in the tree even more. It was useless to try to rush him. Razi did things in his own time.

What Keisha could see was Huff Park. Through a break in the leaves, she followed the boardwalk path through the marsh. Then she found the place where she and Daddy had seen the deer tracks. Two paths crisscrossed through the marsh and over the streambed. She couldn't understand why people would walk on those paths. The marsh was so mucky. They must be animal trails. Near the center of the marsh, a circle of grass had been trampled down. From above, it looked like a big nest among the bushes and little trees that grew out of the muck.

"Careful!" Zeke called from below.

"I hadn't thought of that," Keisha answered back. At the moment, she was feeling just a shade past sassy because she really wanted to be tracking the deer with Daddy.

"Keisha, it's getting late," Daddy said. "And dark, too."

Keisha understood. In a few weeks, the time would change and it would be lighter in the late afternoon for a while, but now it seemed to grow dark so early. She thought hard. How could she get Razi to come down faster?

"Look, Razi, the moon."

"I don't see it."

"You have to come down a branch. Oh, it's a big harvest moon. There's a space down here with me. I bet Wynken and Blynken and Nod are in that moon."

"I want to see Wynken and Blynken." Razi let Keisha guide his foot to the branch just below it.

"Maybe we can get all bundled up and watch the moon from the porch tonight. I'll read you the story."

"Can you see the river of crystal light?" Razi took another step down.

"Not yet, but if we get home in time to help Mama

with supper, maybe we'll see it from the porch."

"I don't like herring fish." Razi was now lost in the story of Wynken and Blynken. Two more branches and they'd be close enough to jump down.

"They're not herring fish, really. Remember? The fish are the stars, and the nets of silver and gold are the last rays of the sun, and the—"

"Hey, next time take us up there," Zack said. He had interlaced his fingers so that Keisha and Razi didn't have to jump but could step right into his hands.

"Yeah, your dad made us stay down here and find something intelligent to say to our mom about tree bark." Zeke held out the piece of bark he'd been studying.

"I don't think there's anything to say about tree bark that isn't boring," Zack said.

"Time to go, kids." Daddy was rubbing his stomach. "In fact, I think it's time for dinner."

"But what about the little deer, Daddy?"

"I'm afraid there isn't much we can do now, Key. There's no sign of him. I'm betting he's found a way to get that pumpkin off his head and he's having a tasty dinner of dried serviceberries and dogwood twigs."

"Yuck," Zeke said. "That's the kind of thing my mom would make for dinner. Can we eat at your house?"

"I'm afraid not, boys. Grandma Alice isn't feeling well and we're expecting that new animal tonight."

"That's right! Is it an owl?" Zeke wanted to know.

"A fox?" Zack guessed.

"Close. It's a coyote pup. Or at least part coyote pup. Big Bob has asked us to figure out how much coyote is in the little guy."

"He might be a doggy," Razi said, stopping on the trail, the corners of his mouth turned down. "A bad doggy."

"He's a puppy," Keisha reminded her brother. She turned to her father. "Do you think we could bundle up after dinner and look at the moon from the screen porch?"

"Please, Daddy! I want to see Wynken and Blynken," Razi said.

"Well, it is a fine harvest moon. We'll see how long it takes to get the new guy settled."

Back at the truck, Daddy reminded the Sanders boys to keep to the sidewalk. "Cars have less visibility at dusk."

"Do you think Big Bob might be there already?" Keisha asked Daddy on the ride home. "I remember him saying 'after dinner.' "

As it turned out, Big Bob couldn't bring over the

new guy until after the Carter children's bedtime. Keisha knew that Mama *knew* how disappointed she was not to be the first to see the puppy. That might have been why Mama let them pull out the sleeping bags on a school night, so they could be cozy and warm while looking at the moon. Even though they were washed and put away for the summer, Daddy got them from the attic and zipped both children into their bags.

Daddy picked up Keisha inside her sleeping bag and placed her on the glider. Then he did the same with Razi. When they were settled, Mama handed them their hot cocoas.

"With all that padding, you look like two hibernating bears," Grandma Alice said. She was still too sore to get into her sleeping bag. And she was cranky that she, too, would be in bed when Big Bob came over later that evening.

"At least put on some socks, Alice," Mama told her. "We don't want you to catch a chill on top of your sore back." Mama held baby Paulo in her arms. He was in his sleep sack. It was as if he slept in a sleeping bag every night.

"I am not going to put a thing on my feet until someone notices."

Razi was the first to guess. "You painted your toes."

"Women don't paint their toes, Razi. They paint their toe*nails*. No. Something else."

"Mom, is that the ring from Big Bob's mother?" Daddy leaned closer to Grandma's foot.

"It's a toe ring," Grandma said. "It's very fashion-forward."

"I don't know if Bob wants his mother's ring on your toe, Mom."

"What would you know about what Bob likes and doesn't like? And besides, what's wrong with my toes?"

"They're bumpy," Razi said. "I'd rather look at the moon. Mama, will you sing 'Wynken and Blynken'?"

Grandma harrumphed and hobbled back into the house.

"She's a crankmeister," Daddy said. "I hope she feels better soon."

The Carter children were quiet for a moment as they settled into their sleeping bags. Keisha listened for the city sounds of cars going by, of people calling out to each other and doors closing and the hum of the electric wires overhead. Razi slurped his hot chocolate.

"Come over here, Fay. I'll be your sleeping bag," Daddy said as he lowered himself into the rocker. Mama sat down on Daddy's lap, cradling baby Paulo, who looked up at her with big, wide eyes. Keisha wondered why babies' eyes seemed to get bigger just before they fell asleep.

Mama started to sing: "Wynken, Blynken, and Nod one night sailed off in a wooden shoe—sailed on a river of crystal light into a sea of dew. 'Where are you going and what do you wish?' the old moon asked the three. . . ."

Keisha knew what she wished. She wished *she* could be the sleeping bag for a puppy. While Mama sang, Keisha asked the old moon if he would take Canis Major, the constellation of stars that Daddy told her was one of Orion's hunting dogs, and turn it into a real dog for her.

Chapter 5

That night, long after bedtime, Keisha had the strangest dream, that the moon asked her what color puppy she wanted and she said that it didn't matter as long as it didn't frighten Razi. And then the moon asked, "Are you sure?" But the way he asked was so strange because he kept repeating himself in a very high voice and he drew the words out: "Are are are you shhhhhhuuuuurrrrr?"

Keisha sat up in bed. She was not afraid of the dark, but it was a little scary to hear the moon still asking his question when her eyes were open. Her dream was not completely a dream.

She put on her slippers, pulled her shawl around her and went out into the hall, following the noises, which led her to the back of the house. The sound got louder as she peered into the dark porch. Keisha thought it was a little like a police siren. But a siren always sounded the same—*woowoowoowoo*—while this noise was more like *arrrrrrrrrooooooooooooo*. Sometimes, at the end, there was a long, drawn-out *rooroorooooooooo*.

Keisha pulled her shawl tighter and stepped into the room. She was surprised to find Mama in the corner, looking out into the darkness.

"Ada," Mama whispered. "Not all our neighbors like living so close to wild animals, even when they are in pens. Someone is going to call the police."

Keisha slipped underneath Mama's arm. "Is that the coyote puppy?"

"Yes. But he does not vocalize like any puppy I have ever known. And now we see why he got the name he did."

Racket was an awful name for a puppy, but Keisha didn't have time to think about puppy names. She had to think about solving this problem. Mama always said Daddy could sleep through a train wreck, and Grandma took a muscle-relaxer pill before she went to bed. This was Mama and Keisha's problem.

"How big is he?" Keisha asked, thinking he must be quite big to make so much noise.

"He's a tiny thing. He must be all lungs inside." Just as Mama said that, the howling stopped. She sighed. "Maybe he's giving up," she said.

"Would he fit in the cat carrier?"

Mama touched the ends of her long fingers to her forehead. "Bob brought him over in one."

"Well, then, let me bring him into my room. Maybe he's just lonely."

"Or maybe it's the moon. Have you ever seen such a big moon? Let's see if he's finished first—"

Ar-ar-arrrrooooooo. The little guy must have paused to collect more night air because this howl seemed louder.

Mama gripped Keisha's arm tight before she let go. "All right. I'll bring him in. Go back to your room."

Keisha ran back to her room on tiptoes, she was so excited. A real puppy in her room! What difference did it make what sort of puppy? Puppies were puppies. You could train a puppy to do just about anything. If you could train a puppy to shake your hand, Keisha bet she and Big Bob and the rest of the 4-H Wild 4-Ever Club could teach Racket not to howl at the moon.

Of course, the smart part of Keisha knew that howling at the moon was not the only thing that stood between her and her lifelong dream of owning her very own puppy, but "first things Fiorenza," as Grandma always said.

"Here." Mama swept in and put the cat carrier down. She had draped her own shawl over the opening, so Keisha couldn't see the puppy.

"No need to get him excited now. He will smell you," Mama whispered. "Keep this cover on and I'll turn out the light. Maybe that will settle him. Good night, Ada."

Mama closed the door behind her and Keisha kept very still for a moment, trying to think what to do next. Animals could sense fear, danger, aggression. She wanted this little puppy to sense warmth, comfort, peace.

He must have sensed *something* because, after a minute, he started to whimper. Keisha thought back to what she had read about coyotes in the animal files. She knew they were related to dogs and that the pups stayed with their mamas in dens for a long time . . . and that Mama caught food and stored it in her stomach and when she got back to the den, she threw it up.

Yuck. That was worse than cold toad-in-the-hole.

The pup yowled. If he made too much noise, Mama would come back in and take him away.

"Oh, don't. Please!" Keisha pulled off the shawl and, for one startled moment, she and the puppy stared at one another. In the darkness, Keisha could just make out two glossy button eyes and one moist nose. She saw a ruff of furry hair and two ears that stuck up so pertly, they looked like the bow tie Grandpa Wally Pops used to wear when he took Grandma Alice out on a date.

Had a puppy ever been this cute?

She didn't care if he was a coyote or a collie or a cross between the two. He was a baby. The cutest little baby she had ever seen.

Keisha had been longing to love a puppy for so many months that she forgot everything Mama told her except to get the pup to settle down.

"First a den nest." Keisha jumped onto her bed, twirling and twisting the bedcovers into a swirl, the way she had seen a fox mama do once with an old sleeping bag.

Then she opened the crate. The puppy shrank back.

"No, sweet thing. I'm going to be your mama." Keisha didn't give the puppy a chance to decide if he wanted a mama. She scooped him up in her arms and took him into bed. She put the puppy in the center of the swirl, curled herself around him and pulled the cover partway over both of them.

"*Roorooroo,*" she said over and over, running her hand over the puppy's back. He stretched out his legs and looked at her with his sparkly eyes. Then he licked her hand.

Keisha was not certain who fell asleep first. Before she knew it, Razi's voice shouting, "No, bad doggy!" ended her sweet slumber.

The poor pup was so surprised, he dove under the covers.

"I was going to crawl into bed with you," Razi said, pouting.

"Razi Carter, I have had it with you!" Keisha sat up and tried to rub the sleep out of her eyes. "The poor little pup was scared half to death last night when Big Bob brought him to this strange place, and for all I know, you scared him whole to death. Out! Now."

"You can't make me because I'm going by *myself*!" Razi answered. Keisha could already see the tears. It served him right. She lifted up the covers and tried to see where the pup had burrowed.

"Keisha, baby, I need your help." While Keisha's head was under the covers, Grandma came in. "I can't find my glasses!"

Keisha poked her head out just in time to see Grandma sit down on the end of the bed.

"It's this ring Bob gave me. I think it got small overnight, but I can't see."

"Where did you leave your glasses?"

"I thought you would know."

Keisha looked for a bulge in Grandma's bathrobe pocket, but the glasses obviously weren't there. "I'm kinda busy right now, Grandma."

"Well, just have a look at my foot. I can't find the ring."

"Grandma, what happened? Your foot is swollen."

"Is that my *foot*?"

Grandma leaned back so she could bring her foot up high enough for Keisha to see. She must have put her hand on the poor little puppy because Keisha heard a squealing, then watched the covers move and the little pup dart out from under the bedclothes and out of the room.

"Grandma! Big Bob's ring is stuck tighter than your guardian angel. And on top of that, now we have a loose coyote pup."

Keisha rushed out the door before Grandma could get herself back up.

For the second time in as many days, Keisha ran into Mama and baby Paulo in the hall.

"Just what do you think you're doing tearing around in your pajamas, miss?"

"I can't explain it now, Mama. Did you by chance see anything small and furry run by here?"

"Don't tell me you opened the door to that crate."

"I promise I won't tell a lie," Keisha answered. "Um . . . have you seen Razi?" she asked, trying to look into his bedroom. But Mama was blocking her view.

"Ada, tell me what happened to that pup."

"Well . . ." Keisha looked at baby Paulo for some inspiration, but all he did was drool and chew on his keys. "The little puppy started to moan and then it started to howl. It was just a little *roorooroo*, but I knew that if it got any louder, you would hear and do something else with it. So I tookitoutofthecrateandsleptwithitinmybed." Keisha hustled that part right along because that was what would get her in hot water. "Anyway, it was *fine*, but then Razi came in and started yelling and then the puppy dove to the end of the bed *and then* Grandma came in and sat on it."

"We may need to have another talk about the right

way to handle wild animals," Mama said, giving Keisha her serious look.

"I'm sorry, Mama. I guess I was exploring the gray area." Daddy liked the gray area more than Mama. It wasn't right; it wasn't wrong. It was a creative solution somewhere in between. "Can I be the one to find him?" Keisha begged. "Please?"

"I think we may have to amputate here unless I get some assistance!" Grandma called from Keisha's bedroom. "I got my foot close enough to my eyes to see that my toe is purple!"

Mama's lips were pressed together in a way that no member of the Carter family liked to see. She preferred mornings to be peaceful, especially before she had her coffee. She held up four fingers. "One, I will see to Grandma; two, you will find your father; three, we will find the pup; and four, we'll all do what we're supposed to do first thing in the morning, and that is get ready for school."

Keisha knew there was no use arguing. And she knew where to find Daddy, so that wouldn't take much time. She ran back to her room. Grandma was lying on Keisha's bed with her feet up in the air. Normally, she called this her L-takes-a-nap pose, but she didn't have the happy expression she usually did when she was doing her gentle yoga poses.

"I'm draining the blood out of my legs to reduce the possibility of digit loss," Grandma said. Keisha grabbed her shawl off the peg and went to the window to look for Daddy. There he was out back doing his morning check. At the moment, there was an eastern screech owl that had gotten tangled in a barbed wire fence, the skinny bunnies and a pigeon that couldn't fly. Keisha tugged on her slippers and ran downstairs, out the back door and down the steps to the wildlife pens.

"Whoa, whoa, whoa!" Daddy said. "Still in your pajamas? Don't tell me you're chasing a loose coyote pup, because I seem to be missing one here."

Keisha jumped into Daddy's arms. Even though she was practically grown, he could still hold her the way he did when they used to play rescue-the-princess-from-the-fire-breathing-dragon. "Daddy, I explored the gray area."

"I knew something was topsy-turvy. When the animals get loose, they don't usually take the crates with them."

"Plus Grandma's toe is purple—the one she put Big Bob's ring on—and Mama wants you to come right now."

"Well, the patients won't be happy about waiting for breakfast, but I guess rescuing Grandma's toe takes priority." Daddy started walking toward the house with

Keisha still in his arms. "Whew. This is hard work. Is it warmer than normal or have you grown again?"

Keisha thought about that. She didn't always like being the second-tallest girl in the class. "It's still warm," she said. "For October."

"Well, there's a cold front coming, according to the weather satellite. We'll have to make sure the pens are snug."

They climbed up the back steps, and Daddy set his eldest child on her feet before opening the door.

"Daddy . . ." Keisha stood inside the house but held her father back from entering. "I think there's more Canis Major than *Canis latrans* in that little puppy. Coyotes are wild animals, but he was happy to sleep in my bed. And that's what domesticated dogs like to do." She stepped aside so Daddy could come in the door, too. "But still, I don't think we should take him back to the Humane Society yet."

"I agree that he has some of the characteristics of a domestic dog, but who's going to want a puppy that howls at the moon? This problem bears further study."

Keisha nodded. Daddy had told her he used that sentence when he wanted to buy time to think things over. Keisha hoped he was thinking along the same lines as she was: a half-wild puppy might be just right for the Carter family.

Upstairs, the baby was rolling around on the bed while Mama examined Grandma's foot.

"Whoa, your foot really is swollen, Mom," Daddy said.

"I think my blood pressure medication needs to be checked again," Grandma said. "My feet are always bigger in the morning."

"But now this ring is stuck tight. Let's keep your foot up, Alice." Mama turned to Daddy. "Fred, will you get me an ice pack? Maybe if we bring a little of the swelling down, we can get it off."

The baby grabbed his own toes, rolling back and forth and giggling.

"Show-off," Grandma said. "I can do the happy baby pose, too, when I'm not injured. Fayola, do you think we can save this toe?"

"I think we can save your toe *and* this pretty ring," Mama said, piling up pillows so Grandma's foot stayed elevated. "Now, Keisha, it is time for number three. Search every room on this floor. I don't know where your brother has disappeared to, but tell him to bring me the liquid soap from the bathroom. Maybe we can get Grandma's toe slippery enough to slide off the ring."

Keisha walked slowly down the hall, peering first into the bathroom and Paulo's dark room before she looked into Razi's.

"Razi, you need to help Ma—" Keisha stopped short in the doorway. There was Razi sitting on the bed and holding Racket out at arm's length.

"I found your puppy, Key," he said.

Keisha rushed over. You held a puppy so that his hind feet were supported. Dangling in the air like that made an animal feel vulnerable. Keisha took Racket into her arms like a baby and cooed to him. He licked her face.

"Razi, how—"

"I was under the bed and then I felt something. I thought it was you because you're the only one who fits under there, too. And then I got some wet on my neck and then I said, 'Key, uck, don't kiss me,' and then I turned around and it was your puppy. I started to say, 'Bad doggy,' and then before I did he licked my nose." Razi smiled at the memory. "And then he licked all over my face!"

"See, Razi? Every dog is not a bad dog."

Keisha and Razi looked at the puppy. One of his ears flopped forward. His little tongue lolled out at the side. He was the opposite of bad doggy. He was adorable doggy. Keisha turned him over and placed him on her lap.

"Do you want to pet him?"

Razi sat on his hands, all of a sudden remembering his fear of dogs. He shook his head.

"Do you want to watch me pet him?"

Razi nodded yes.

After a moment of serious stroking, Racket stretched out again. Keisha tickled her fingers behind his ears. Before long, one hand crept out from beneath Razi's thigh, and he began making little taps on Racket's behind.

Keisha heard Daddy coming up the stairs with the ice pack. Razi shouted: "Daddy, come see. I'm petting the doggy. I'm not afraid!"

The sound of Daddy's work boots clomping on the wood floor, combined with Razi's shouting, startled Racket. He wriggled out of Keisha's hands and dove under the bed again.

"What a scaredy-coyote," Keisha said. She got down on her hands and knees to search for the puppy.

"So we've found our little runaway?" Keisha heard Daddy's voice behind her.

"We did, but then the sound of your footsteps scared him," she said.

"That's our second D.I.D. this week."

Keisha thought for a moment. "Oh, right. Dog in Distress. Don't forget our G.I.D."

Daddy held up the ice pack. "Right. I'm on my way to our Grandma in Distress."

Chapter 6

Had a school day *ever* gone so slowly? During math, Keisha made up story problems about how little difference it would make to add one coyote pup to the feeding schedule. Everyone worked extra hard in social studies because Mr. Drockmore had decided to let them do their oral reports in any costume they wanted. The extra-credit points would still be given, but they would be based on costume creativity. Keisha was almost as happy as Aaliyah that she didn't have to wear the funny hat and the apron in front of the whole school. Since her report was already written, Keisha spent her social studies time rereading Phillis Wheatley's poetry to see if she ever mentioned dogs. In art, she pressed her clay eraser into the shape of a puppy head with ears that stuck up and little button eyes. What a relief to get to the end of the school day and use up some of her puppy-wanting energy in jump rope practice.

Usually they practiced in the multi-purpose room, but the janitor was polishing the floor, so they had to share the gym with the boys' basketball team. In all the confusion made by boys and basketballs, they couldn't count out their jumps to synchronize, so Mr. Rose just had them practice speed jumping and double unders. Keisha jumped until her heart thumped as fast as she swung the rope. Between sets, she told Aaliyah and Wen what had happened the night before.

"So let me get this straight . . . ," Aaliyah said after they started another set (Aaliyah was the only one who could talk while jumping). "You want us to help you figure out how to get your mama—not an average mama who doesn't already have lots of animals to take care of, like Wen's or mine, but *your* mama—to let you keep a puppy that howls at the moon loud enough for the whole neighborhood to hear?"

Mr. Rose blew the whistle, signaling the end of practice.

Keisha stopped jumping. She nodded her head. "In addition to being adorable," she panted, "he's the only puppy Razi's not afraid of. It's my best chance."

Wen sat sideways on the bleachers, hugging her knees. Keisha noticed that one of Wen's socks had fallen down to her ankle while she was jumping.

"I guess we can't use the guard dog argument," Wen said. "If he's afraid of your daddy's boots and Razi's screaming."

"But he is so cute!" Keisha pulled a mat back out on the floor to get the gym ready for Mr. Rose's K–2 class the next day. "When he cuddles up with me and stretches out his legs and licks my hand . . . ooh, he's the canine version of baby Paulo."

Aaliyah was not convinced. "You'd have to have a reason like . . . his howling woke up the family and saved you from a fire, to convince your mama."

Keisha chose to ignore Aaliyah for the moment. "Your socks, Wen. Then help me with this big mat, will you?"

Aaliyah left them to drop all the coiled ropes into the jump rope bin. Before Wen grabbed the royal blue mat, she lined up her socks just right. The two girls dragged the mat into place. Keisha fell on it and did a somersault. So did Wen. They met in the middle.

"Do you think it's impossible?" Keisha whispered, taking Wen's hands and starting a "Miss Lucy" handclap.

"Nei-Nei says nothing is impossible," Wen said, referring to her wise grandmother. "Some goals are just harder to reach than others."

"How do I reach getting a puppy of my own? Now that I've slept curled up next to one, I want him more than ever."

"Well, Aaliyah's right that your mama will be the hardest one to convince. What does *she* think is important? Maybe if we looked at it that way."

Wen and Keisha had been hand-clapping since kindergarten. They didn't need to say the words to know the clap. They could clap to anything.

Keisha thought hard for a moment. Mama cared about her family. She cared about the business. She cared about being a good neighbor.

"How about if I go home and do this?" Keisha stopped clapping and put her hands in her lap. It was their signal to begin again.

> "I need a puppy, puppy, puppy
> All dressed in fur, fur, fur
> To keep my brother, brother, brother
> Out of the Peaceful Corner-ner-ner."

Aaliyah scooched in next to them and they started to do the handclap again. With three girls, it was a lot more complicated. It had taken them all the way to third grade to get it just right. Aaliyah chanted loudly:

> "Here comes Marcus, Marcus, Marcus,
> All dressed in red, red, red.
> He likes the ribbon, ribbon, ribbon
> That's on your head, head, head."

Basketball practice was ending, too, and Marcus dribbled over to the girls. "What did you just say about me, Aaliyah?" he asked.

"I almost forgot," Wen said, trying to rescue Keisha from potentially the most embarrassing situation ever. "When Marcus and I read *It's the Great Pumpkin, Charlie Brown* this morning to the first graders, Razi kept telling everyone that a deer took his trick-or-treat pumpkin."

"Yeah, what was that about?" Marcus kept dribbling.

Boom. Boom. Between the legs. *Boom. Boom.*

"Well . . ." Keisha figured it couldn't hurt to tell her friends. Zeke and Zack knew, and they were as bad as Mr. Sanders about keeping secrets.

She proceeded to fill Wen, Aaliyah and Marcus in on the latest rescue effort.

"I don't understand," Wen said when Keisha finished. "Tell me again."

"We thought the picture Mr. Gorman took would help us solve the mystery of why the pumpkin was stuck so tight, but when we blew it up on our computer at home, it was out of focus. Daddy and I figured that the only way was if the handle was over the deer's head."

"I don't get it, either," Marcus said. "Those handles aren't long. How could it stretch?"

Keisha started to explain that they'd done some measuring with Razi's trick-or-treat pumpkin and the handle wouldn't have to stretch that far, but she was interrupted by Mr. Rose blowing his whistle. That meant the school would close in five minutes.

"So what are you going to be for Halloween, Marcus?" Aaliyah asked. "You won't get any creativity points for being a basketball player."

"Maybe I don't need extra-credit points in social studies." Marcus tried to spin his basketball on the tip of his finger, but it fell off. He chased it to the corner of the gym.

"I'm set on a Romany," Keisha said. "But we've only got two days to come up with a costume."

"Well, I think a red-carpet celebrity will win me points." Aaliyah pulled on her sweater. "Especially if I can find a good way to roll the carpet out and roll it up again."

"Just don't make it so complicated we can't run," Keisha said. The other kids nodded, remembering the most important rule of Halloween—collect candy!

"Is Keisha Carter still here?" Ms. Tellerico asked in her assembly voice as she came through the big double doors.

Keisha stood up and whirled around, almost bumping into Marcus.

Marcus did two more dribbles. *Boom. Boom.* "Uh-oh," he said. "The principal's looking for you."

Ms. Tellerico spotted Keisha and waved. "Keisha, I'm so glad you're still here. I've just been talking to Mrs. Jenkins. Will you please deliver this letter to your parents?"

"Even the super-squeezy concentration ball didn't help?" Wen whispered as they headed to the corner of the gym for their coats. "Poor Razi."

Marcus faded back for one more jump shot into the big bin that held all the balls. "Score! Did you see that, Key?" he shouted when the ball landed right on top of the pile.

Keisha smiled as she put the letter in her backpack. It felt as if Marcus was showing off a little just for her.

As Keisha and Wen came out of the school, they heard the familiar *brrring brrring* of Big Bob's bicycle bell.

"I was hoping we'd catch you." Big Bob was pumping the pedals, and Keisha's friend Jorge was sitting on the handlebars. "We just finished setting up for tomorrow's Wild 4-Ever meeting. Want company on your walk home, Keisha?"

"Hey, Key." Jorge waved.

Big Bob's bike had two baskets mounted on the back. He tried to do all his shopping on his bike when the weather was good. Jorge had put his backpack in one of the baskets. Keisha dumped hers in the other and walked alongside the bike.

Big Bob pedaled slow and easy, keeping to the sidewalk. People stepped aside when they saw the three of them coming.

"Sooooo," he said after they'd been going along for a while. "How does Alice like her ring?"

"She likes it," Keisha said.

"Have you seen her wear it?"

"She never takes it off," Keisha said.

"Oh, I'm so glad. I was worried that it wouldn't be her style. What finger does she wear it on? Did it fit her ring finger or is she wearing it on her pinky?"

Keisha hoped the whistling wind would make "piggy" sound like "pinky."

But Big Bob stopped his bike at the corner and said, "Piggy?"

For an old guy, he had excellent hearing.

"She put my mother's ring on her *toe*?"

"Well, Grandma says toe rings are even more fashion-forward than pinky rings," Keisha replied, trying to sound convincing as she stopped beside the bike. "She saw it on the Look On-line."

Jorge and Big Bob got off the bike, and they continued up the street to the Carters' house. Big Bob said, "There's something about my mother's ring on Alice's toe that does not feel right to me."

Jorge grabbed his backpack and handed Keisha hers. They walked the rest of the way in silence, interrupted only by Harvey's barking as they passed the Bakers' house.

"The thing is . . ." Keisha took one step up to the Carters' front porch. "It's stuck."

"Stuck as in . . ."

"Stuck as in stuck tight. When I left this morning, Mama had Grandma's foot up high with an ice pack, so maybe it's off by now."

"My mother's ring on Alice's toe." Bob looked at the passersby on the street with wonder. "Maybe I won't visit today, with Alice so under the weather and all. But here's something to try. Whenever one of the girls got a ring stuck on her finger, my mother used vegetable oil. Good old vegetable oil. It worked every time."

Jorge looked at Keisha. Then he dropped his backpack back in Big Bob's bike basket. But Big Bob was hesitating. "So . . . ," he said. "How's it going with the pup, by the way?"

"Oh, okay." Keisha wasn't sure what to tell Big Bob. If he knew Mama was worried the puppy might hurt their standing in the neighborhood, he'd definitely take Racket back. "I think the problem bears further study," Keisha said.

"I've been doing some studying, too, about the difference between wild and domesticated animals. Wild animals are more aggressive. They have to defend themselves and their territory to survive. Domesticated animals are more likely to cooperate. They have to learn to live close together with their own and different species."

"Racket's definitely not aggressive," Keisha said.

"No, he's very submissive. But a vet who lives out in the country responded to Dr. Wendy's request with a lot of information about coydogs. Most of them don't make good pets because they're more likely to bite, the way wild animals are supposed to. But every once in a while, he finds one that has no aggression at all."

"So does that mean Racket would be a good pet?" Keisha asked.

"Well, we can't forget that he howls at the moon *and* he's too young for us to know what other parts of him are coyote-like. Coyotes are big hunters. Another vet on the Listserv talked about a coydog that hunted the cats in the neighborhood."

"You mean . . ."

Big Bob nodded. "Cat fillet."

"Can I see the coydog?" Jorge asked.

Keisha was still shocked. *Racket eat a cat?*

She looked at Jorge, trying to remember what he'd just said. Finally, she snapped out of it. "I think that would be okay." Leading the way around the side of the house, Keisha took the path back to the animal pens. Racket's cage was empty.

Had Mama sent him back to the Humane Society already?

"Let me check inside a minute," she said to Jorge and Big Bob. But before she reached the back steps, Keisha saw a flash of bow-tie ears followed by a boy in a superhero cape. Razi was running and giggling.

"I got you!" he said. Then he shouted, "Big Bob!" Razi forgot all about Racket and ran over to give Big Bob a hug.

"What's going on here?" Big Bob asked, holding a delighted Razi up in the air.

"First, Racket got scared by the oven door and I had to find him. And then Racket got scared by Mr. Sanders coming over to hear about the poor deer and have a bowl of soup, and I had to find him *again*. And then Racket got scared by the radio in the car going by, and I was just finding him when you came by to visit."

"My goodness," Big Bob said, putting Razi down and patting him on the shoulder. "What isn't Racket scared of?"

"Me!" Razi grabbed both corners of his superhero cape, and it caught the breeze. "But I had to become Find-It Man to get him the last time. Jorge!" Razi saw Jorge and gave him a big hug, too.

Keisha noticed Mama on the back steps without her coat on, hugging herself and smiling.

"Help me, Jorge." Razi took Jorge's hand. "Even Find-It Man needs help." Jorge let himself be led to the back of the yard. Keisha was about to chase after the boys, but she remembered the letter Ms. Tellerico had given her. She unzipped her backpack.

"That is the Razi *I* know," Mama said. "Creative, full of life . . . happy."

"Did he come home unhappy again, Mama?"

"Why do you ask, Ada?"

"Because Ms. Tellerico gave me this note to give you."

Big Bob asked Mama if he could say a quick hello to Alice.

"Of course, Bob." Mama frowned at the envelope.

"Hey, Bob." Daddy appeared in the doorway and stood aside for Big Bob to pass through.

"Did you find the deer, Daddy?"

"Not yet, Key. I did find some fresh tracks on that trail, so I know the deer are still using it."

Razi and Jorge ran back from the pens, and Keisha and Mama and Daddy watched as Razi dove under the bushes at the side of the house.

"Razi Carter!" Mama scolded. "You will get your cape all dirty, not to mention your shoes, your—"

Jorge ran up the steps and said quietly to Mama, "One of the rabbit babies has disappeared. Razi said there were three. The cage wasn't latched and Razi is afraid you'll blame him."

Mama folded the envelope and put it in her apron pocket. "A rabbit baby on the loose and a coyote puppy, too. If this doesn't spell disaster—" Mama broke off and looked at Keisha.

"I found him! He was under the bushes." Razi

dragged Racket out from underneath the yews. Both the boy and the dog would need the dust swatted off them before entering the house.

So Razi found one of the animals. But what about the bunny?

Keisha didn't have a chance to think it through because Big Bob came to the door and said, "Alice is watching the news, and they announced that next up is a story about a deer with a pumpkin stuck on its head."

Chapter 7

Mama didn't see much use for television, but Grandma said if she couldn't watch shows like *What Your Shoes Say About You* and *Celebrity Slips*, life wasn't worth living. So the only television in the Carters' house was in Grandma's bedroom.

In the time it took to get through the commercials, the Carter family plus Big Bob and Jorge were gathered around Grandma's small set.

Grandma whispered to Keisha as she came in, "Go get the Sunset Glow lipstick from my makeup bag. I don't have my face on!"

Before she left for the bathroom, Keisha noticed that Grandma had covered her swollen foot with her cashmere sweater.

As soon as Racket saw Keisha, he began whining and straining to get out of Razi's arms.

"Keisha, sit with the puppy on the floor," Mama said. "You can see better from there, anyway."

Racket jumped up on Keisha, giving her a thorough face wash before he stretched out on her lap and sighed. He seemed happy to be found.

The commercials ended, and a dark-haired woman

with a ponytail looked into the camera with a serious expression. "Coming up next . . . will this deer survive? Our *Live at Five* Action Team received an e-mail this morning about a young deer in peril right here in one of our city parks. Our exclusive footage . . . after these messages."

"Well, I guess they found it," Daddy said as a toothpaste tube played the keys of a piano that turned into some very white teeth. "I wonder if the e-mail came from Mr. Gorman's phone. Razi did send the photo to his whole list."

"They may have found it, but that doesn't mean they caught it." Big Bob settled himself at Grandma's side on the bed. "That's the tricky part. Speaking of tricky parts . . . Alice, what do I hear about my mother's—"

"Shhh," Grandma said. "She's back."

All eyes returned to the television.

"Mindy Patel here, your *Live at Five* Action Team correspondent. Earlier today, our news bureau's information center was alerted to the plight of a young deer that went for a nibble and got more than he bargained for."

The photo that Razi, Keisha, Daddy and the Z-Team had seen on Mr. Gorman's camera phone flashed up on the screen.

"So we came down to the park to sniff out the story. Here's what we know. This pumpkin is stuck fast and the little deer can't drink or eat. How could this happen? Let's go to the neighbors who alerted us."

Two people, a lady and Mr. Gorman, were escorted in front of the camera. Mindy Patel took a step toward them and continued speaking.

"Ms. Dunwoody was the first to spot the deer. In your own words, will you tell us what happened?"

"I was getting ready for work when I saw this poor, poor deer with its head stuck in the little pumpkin I fill with sunflower seeds for the birds."

"And then . . ."

"It's an 'and then' story!" Razi shouted. Razi loved "and then" stories.

"Well, I looked up 'wildlife' in the phone book and I found the number for Carters' Urban Rescue. And I spoke to a girl who said she'd tell her father. That was it. I had to rush to get the bus."

"A little girl working for a wildlife rescue operation?" Mindy Patel looked at the camera with a quizzical face. "That sounds dangerous to—"

"I met those young people," Mr. Gorman interrupted Mindy Patel. "They were with their father. It was all perfectly safe. The little one sent you that photograph. Though how he did it—"

By the look on Mindy Patel's face, Keisha could see she did not like to be interrupted. "So you're saying *you're* the one who reported this tragedy, Mr. Gorman."

"Don't go blaming me. It was the little guy. I just took the photo because, well, at the time it seemed kinda funny and I thought I'd send it to my grandbaby who's in the hospital right now. Hey there, Tracyanne junior."

Mr. Gorman waved to the camera until Mindy Patel caught him by the arm.

"A little guy sent the photo. Is this whole operation run by children?"

During Mindy Patel's second thoughtful look at the camera, Grandma broke out with "Jeez Louis Vuitton. Stick to the story."

"No, no," Mr. Gorman was saying. "They were with their father when they—"

"What we *do* know," Mindy Patel broke in, "is that they did *not* find the deer because only moments ago, our *Live at Five* Action Team took this footage."

The television screen showed a blurry scene of leaves and trees, accompanied by the sound of snapping twigs. The lens zoomed in, and viewers got a fleeting glimpse of the floating pumpkin that was indeed stuck tight over the nose and mouth of a young deer.

After a few shaky seconds of the deer in distress, a serious Mindy Patel's face reappeared. "And I must say that I, for one, would rather see children running a lemonade stand than chasing after wild animals."

"They weren't chasing anything . . . ," Mr. Gorman said. "They were tracking with their—"

Mindy Patel walked a few steps away and was

followed by the camera. "Earlier today, we were able to get our zoo director to comment on the situation. Mr. Vescolani, can this deer be saved?"

The view switched to Mr. Vescolani standing outside the polar bear pen at the zoo, his tie flapping in the breeze. "Well, obviously, catching deer with pumpkins stuck on their heads is a little outside our area of expertise. We're a zoo. Frankly, if I were having this problem, I'd call my friends at Carters' Urban Rescue."

"Well, at least *someone* is talking some kind of sense," Grandma said. Grandma always talked to the TV.

"Could this capture involve guns? Don't you knock out wild animals with dart guns?"

"Dart guns are a dangerous business. About half the wild animals that size will die of complications when anesthetized. You have to get the amount just right. If it's not enough, animals get overexcited and may injure themselves. If it's too much—"

"Could this deer be dangerous to any of our citizens?" Mindy Patel asked Mr. Vescolani. "If he's found and he gets overexcited?"

"He's just a young buck with a pumpkin stuck tight because the handle is caught on his horn buds. I don't see him presenting much danger to the public."

This seemed to disappoint Mindy Patel. Maybe danger was better than safety when you were reporting the news.

The screen showed Mindy Patel again as she said, "Thank you, Mr. Vescolani. Our viewers can follow the story moment by moment on the blog at *Live at Five*'s Action Team news center Web site. Log on and record your comments on this most unusual event. From Huff Park, this is Mindy Patel, your *Live at Five* Action Team correspondent."

As the camera pulled back from the scene at the park and the dramatic music played, Keisha could hear the office phone ringing downstairs. She wasn't surprised. She even had an idea about who would be on the other end of the line.

Handing off a sleepy Racket to Razi, she ran downstairs to answer the phone.

"Carters' Urban Rescue."

"It's time to put our damage-control plan into place," Aaliyah said.

Daddy called Aaliyah the director of marketing for Carters' Urban Rescue. When Aaliyah grew up, she wanted to be an agent who represented singers and athletes. Both of her parents were in marketing, so she talked a lot about visibility and public perceptions and targeted media efforts. Aaliyah never missed the news.

"Just remember that no publicity is bad publicity," she continued. "It's all in how you spin it."

Keisha felt a tap on her shoulder. It was Jorge. "Can you tell me where the vegetable oil is?" he asked.

"In the kitchen, in the cupboard above the sink," Keisha told him, holding her hand over the receiver so she didn't interrupt Aaliyah.

A minute later, Jorge rushed past her and headed upstairs with the Carters' jug of canola oil. He almost ran into Big Bob coming down the stairs. Aaliyah was still talking strategy.

Big Bob told Keisha, "As soon as Jorge delivers that vegetable oil, I've got to get him home. Your mom asked that you come back up when you're done. She needs help with the patient."

"*Hellooooo,*" Aaliyah said. She must have heard Big Bob. "Back to the strategy meeting. Maybe you should practice answering the phone with a deeper voice or something."

All Keisha could manage was a wave to let Big Bob know she'd heard.

"And you need a script by the phone," Aaliyah continued.

"How can you have a script when every call is different?" Keisha wanted to know.

"Ouch!" Grandma shouted so loud, Keisha heard it all the way down the stairs. "Just cut it off! That would be less painful."

The next thing Keisha heard sounded like a dog in distress. *Yowp!*

There were some words from Daddy she couldn't make out and then Razi crying out: "I didn't step on his tail. He put it under my foot!"

Aaliyah kept talking about damage control. If Carters' Urban Rescue had a Web presence, their blog could *at least* respond to the news center's blog.

Keisha watched as Racket dashed down the stairs and into the living room. Razi came after. More skittering puppy. More Razi tears.

"Got it!" Daddy yelled.

"Count my toes," Grandma insisted. "And get that ring away from me. I don't ever want to see it again!"

"I can't find him!" Razi shouted to everyone upstairs.

There was something about this not-Tallahassee day that was making Keisha feel more sassy than classy.

"Aaliyah, maybe *you* can go on the news center blog and make a post. I can't worry about that now. Grandma's in pain, Razi's crying, the puppy's lost again and we have forty-seven math problems due by tomorrow! Right now, I have to do damage control at 180 Horton Street!"

Chapter 8

The Carters' definition of a bad day went something like this:

- An animal in their care died.
- Someone dropped by unexpectedly and no food had been prepared.
- Someone other than Razi or Paulo cried.
- Grandma couldn't draw any positive energy.

The night they got the ring off Grandma's toe, she was in too much pain to draw any positive energy. *Plus* it was like she was mad at Big Bob because *she* put his mother's ring on her toe. Now she wouldn't even wear it on her pinky finger. The bunny was just lost, not dead—yet. There was enough food for drop-ins, and no one other than Razi or Paulo cried, but the family business had not gotten such a good report from Mindy Patel.

It certainly wasn't the worst day in Carter family history, but it wasn't tops, either.

When something bad happened during the day, the Carters tried to feel better about it before going to bed.

Sometimes it worked if they played a little cooperative Scrabble. Everyone showed their tiles and thought of words that helped the other players make big scores. The competition part was that the whole family worked together to beat their highest score.

To increase their chance of happy feelings even more, Mama had found an extra Scrabble game at the Goodwill. She gave that set of tiles to Razi so he could stack them under the kitchen table while she and Grandma and Daddy and Keisha played together.

It was understood that until at least three rounds had been played, no one would mention Racket, who had been found wedged into Grandma's recliner; or the deer in distress; or the "wretched ring," as Grandma called it.

There was the quiet clicking of tiles both above and under the table for several minutes. Soon, half the board was filled with interesting words, like "amble" and "mauve."

"Look, Keisha," Daddy said. "If I

put 'needle' on this double word score, it will set you up to put 'zen' on the triple word score."

" 'Zen' isn't allowed," Mama said. "It's a proper noun."

"I was using it as a regular old noun. As in, we need a little more zen around here," Daddy said.

Grandma used that word a lot. Keisha thought it meant "peaceful." Keisha was kneading Racket's tired body with her feet. Touching puppy fur with your toes was an excellent way to feel zen.

Mama shook her head no.

Keisha said, "Okay, what about 'hex'? That would be even better."

She put the letters H-E-X on the triple word score and counted up the points.

"Maybe if we put a hex on the deer, we could make him stand still long enough to get the pumpkin off his head," she said.

"Bert Vescolani called our cell while you were on the phone with Aaliyah," Daddy told Keisha. "We agreed to go together tomorrow to see if we can locate the little guy. Then we'll decide if it's time to take the risk and tranquilize him."

It was Mama's turn. "Alice, if I put 'star' here, can you make a word that could hit this triple word score?"

"Speaking of letters," Grandma said, "what did your letter say? The one you got from Ms. Tellerico?"

Mama glanced under the table. The rest of the family did, too. Razi was talking to himself and making a circle of letter tiles.

"We need to have a conference about one of our cubs." Mama talked about Razi like an animal baby when she didn't want him to catch on to what she was saying.

"And what did one of our cubs do now?"

"I don't think it's any one thing. It's a pattern."

"Have you ever known our cub to sit still all day?" Daddy asked. "You can make 'starry,' Mom."

"That's not good enough for a triple word score. We need to use the F and the Z."

"Hmmm. What about 'fuzz'? 'Fizz'?"

"There's only one Z. How about 'faze'? I'll wait to see what I pick up next turn."

"I just wish it held his interest more—the cub's, I mean," Daddy said. "If only they got more exercise and did projects with their um . . . paws, like the kids do with Big Bob. Our cub needs a lot of that."

"Maybe Big Bob should start a school for cubs," Mama said.

Everyone was quiet, imagining the possibilities

of spending all day with Big Bob and also thinking about F and Z words that didn't need another Z in them.

The next morning, Keisha came down to the table and found Razi sitting in his pajamas and tearing his French toast into strips. Grandma was at the range flipping bread. Even though she hobbled a little bringing Keisha her plate, it was good to see Grandma outside her bedroom.

"I'm going to be Find-It Man today and find the missing bunny," Razi declared.

"No you're not," Keisha said. "You're going to school." Mama did not allow her children to stay home from school unless they were throwing up or they had a fever.

"No he's not," Grandma said. "He's going to be Find-It Man." Grandma set Keisha's plate down and stood back to examine her. "And I'm going to be Fix-It Girl. Stand up."

Keisha stood up. Grandma tugged on her sweater, refolded the collar of her blouse and pushed Keisha's hair behind her ears. "Better," Grandma declared. "Now you won't ruin my reputation for high fashion at Langston Hughes Elementary."

"Where are Mama and Daddy and baby Paulo?" Keisha asked.

"They're at school."

Keisha wondered if the world had turned upside down while she slept.

Grandma added more steaming French toast to the platter on the table. "In her letter, Ms. Tellerico invited your mama and your dad to a breakfast meeting. Speaking of breakfast, you need to finish yours 'toot-sweet' so you're not late for school."

Though it felt strange to walk to school without her brother, it was kind of nice, too, to be able to get started at the right time and think her own thoughts on the way. Keisha listened to the sound of her feet as they *shush-shush-shush*ed through the leaves on the sidewalk. As she walked, Keisha thought back over all the things that had happened in the last two days. She wished she could think of a good way to catch the deer without hurting him.

Most of the animals they received were either injured and easily caught or small enough to be trapped in a cage. If she could come up with a brilliant idea and post it on the *Live at Five* Action Team Web site, then maybe Mindy Patel would think twice about saying kids shouldn't help with animal rehabilitation. It was so not true. Even Razi helped feed the animal babies.

As Keisha stood on the edge of the playground,

watching all the kids lining up for class—Zack and Zeke, Wen, Aaliyah, Jorge—she thought: *Kids have always been part of Carters' Urban Rescue. Even non-Carter kids.*

Wait a minute.

Daddy often said that two heads were better than one.

What about thirty-two heads? Keisha ran across the blacktop to join her class. "Mr. Drockmore?" She tugged on her teacher's sleeve as they filed in. "Do you think we could do something different during science today?"

"Have you read the blog?" Aaliyah called to Keisha from the line.

"Aaliyah," Mr. Drockmore said. "Keisha and I were talking."

But Aaliyah couldn't stop herself. She was too excited. She rushed over to Keisha and Mr. Drockmore. "There have been fifty-four posts. Everyone is weighing in . . . on kids in family businesses, on nature taking its course. There have been responses from as far away as Taiwan! People want to know what's going to happen if—"

"Ms. Johnson. Please get back in line. There is a time and a place for social conversation."

"Mr. Drockmore," Aaliyah said, putting her hands on her hips. Keisha could see her friend was about to get sassy. "This is *not* social con—"

"Aaliyah," Keisha interrupted. "Please! I need to talk to Mr. Drockmore about this D.I.D."

Aaliyah sighed and took her place in line.

After Keisha finished explaining her idea to Mr. Drockmore, he crossed his arms and drummed his fingers on his sleeve.

"I like it," he said finally. "This is one of those teachable moments when our FFGs can actually see how science is applied to real-world problems." Mr. Drockmore smiled to himself.

"Yes, sir." Keisha patted Mr. Drockmore's arm. "And we might save a baby deer, too."

During science lab, Mr. Drockmore asked the children to close their observation notebooks. He drew an oval with four sticks coming out beneath it on the whiteboard. Then he drew a circle on top and two little ears. Keisha realized it was the baby deer.

"You may have seen the news story last night about the young deer with the pumpkin caught on his head. Like many problems we experience in our everyday lives, I believe this one, too, can be solved by scientific reasoning."

Marcus raised his hand. "But don't you have to catch it before you can reason with it?" he asked. "I thought they said they could get the pumpkin off if they could catch it."

Mr. Drockmore stood back and considered his drawing. "I could use a hand with this drawing, Marcus."

Marcus jumped up and grabbed a dry-erase marker.

"Yes, catching the deer is one problem. That is what everyone else is focusing on. But my question is how this pumpkin can get unstuck *without* catching the deer, since that result seems so unlikely.

"We've been talking all year about creating if-then hypotheses. What are some questions we might ask about how this little deer can separate itself from the pumpkin, questions that could lead us to create a working hypothesis?"

Mr. Drockmore waited for volunteers. Isolde raised her hand. "We could ask what the deer can use . . . like maybe a sharp rock or stick?"

Isolde stopped. She was thinking.

"Keep going, Isolde."

"I was just wondering, how smart is a deer? Can he think about what to use? It wouldn't matter what he had if he didn't know how to—"

"He's smart enough to get Carters' Urban Rescue coverage in Taiwan!" Aaliyah jumped in. "This story is viral! People are sending the deer's picture all over the place. I Googled it this morning and got 427 hits!"

"Aaliyah, do I need to remind you how the scientific process works? Interrupting is not part of the process."

"I'm just trying to explain the process of a media frenzy," Aaliyah said. "For those who might be interested."

"Sometimes, friend Aaliyah, I believe you have what is called a one-track mind." Mr. Drockmore went to the Welcome Wall, where cutout handprints of the whole class were displayed. He placed his hand on his own handprint. On the first day of school, he told his Fantastic Fifth Graders that this was an excellent way to calm down and refocus.

Mr. Drockmore turned to face the class again. "Jorge, do you have any thoughts?"

"Well . . ." Jorge paused. "About what Isolde said . . . Big Bob told me that when deer are really hungry, they do all kinds of stuff for food. That means they can be creative. I bet the little deer is doing everything she can to get that pumpkin off by herself."

"Excellent point." While Jorge was speaking,

Mr. Drockmore had turned his attention back to the board. Marcus had made the pumpkin into a basketball and was drawing a Detroit Pistons jersey on the little deer.

"Thank you, Marcus. That is enough."

Marcus signed his name in flowy handwriting underneath his creation.

"I think we are at the point where we can make some predictions. Open your notebooks, please, and strategize in writing for me. Under what conditions could a deer with no hands and no sharp instruments, such as a knife or scissors, remove a pumpkin from its head?"

"Even if we figure it out," Marcus said as he took his seat, "how do we tell the deer?"

Keisha twisted the eraser on her pencil. Marcus was so funny. She opened her notebook and started to think about an if-then hypothesis. *If* a deer had a pumpkin stuck on its head, *then* it would be very unhappy!

Duh.

She needed to look at this problem from a different angle. It was like Mr. Drockmore said—everyone kept focusing on catching the deer. Was there a way to help it *without* catching it?

Keisha decided to apply "transfer of knowledge" to the project. Mr. Drockmore had taught them that learning something in one area of your life could help you solve a problem in another area, even if all the conditions weren't the same.

Her most recent experience of things being stuck was, of course, Big Bob's ring on Grandma's toe. To get the ring off, they'd tried elevating Grandma's foot, putting ice on it, getting it wet, using soap, using oil, twisting. But none of these things made sense for a baby deer to do without help.

Keisha chewed on her pencil eraser and let her mind wander, imagining the little deer and all the ways it had probably tried to get the pumpkin off already. Once, when Aaliyah tied a ribbon around the neck of Moms's cat Bella, she scooched backward and rolled and bit at the ribbon until she got it off.

"Okay, guys . . ." Mr. Drockmore clapped his hands. "Time to share your observations with a partner."

Keisha looked around for Wen. But Aaliyah was faster. She pushed her chair over to Keisha.

"There's only one way this can work. *You* have to find that baby deer."

"Why me?"

"Because Mindy Patel blamed you and Razi for not doing a good-enough job. You have to prove her wrong."

"Aaliyah, proving Mindy Patel wrong wasn't our assignment. Besides, if Daddy and Mr. Vescolani don't find the deer today, how am I supposed to?"

"Don't ask me. I'm the public-relations girl. Tracking animals is your business."

Mr. Drockmore clapped his hands once more. Time to change partners. Keisha brought her chair to the corner of the room where Wen was frowning at her notebook.

"We need to get the weather forecast," Wen said. "Nei-Nei said we can eat the Brussels sprouts soon, and Brussels sprouts taste best after the first hard frost."

"Okay, now you've lost me." Wen was good at explaining, so Keisha waited.

"We saw it yesterday. The temperature outside things affects their properties. Water in cold temperatures is different than water in hot temperatures. So is plastic. Deer live outside. When the temperature drops, the deer's body will keep him from freezing, but the plastic could freeze if we get a hard frost."

Keisha thought about that. Grandma's ring was

made of metal, so it was already hard. How would it be different if the plastic pumpkin was hard instead of bendy? Wait a minute. With a hard frost and a little help . . .

"Wen," she said. "We *do* need to check the weather. I think I have a hypothesis that might work."

Chapter 9

After school, Keisha sat at the kitchen table and pretended to do math problems. What she was really working on was her if-then hypothesis, but she didn't think Mama would like it much, since it involved Carter children (specifically Keisha) doing dangerous things. Mama sat next to Keisha, figuring out the bills for the month. For every expense, there was an envelope—groceries, water, electricity. Any leftover money went in the envelope marked "extra." The first time she went shopping each month, Mama paid all her bills in cash at the Family Fare service counter. Keisha had tried to explain to Mama about online banking, but Mama said she liked to do things the old-fashioned way and pay her bills with dollars and cents.

Sometimes, working on the envelopes got Mama talking about charging the people who dropped off squirrels with broken legs and songbirds who'd run into picture windows.

Keisha could tell that Mama was thinking that very thing because she looked up from her work and said, "Right now, your father is chasing all over the park after a deer that won't bring in a penny, and I'm to figure out how much extra it will cost if Razi goes to a new school."

"A new school?"

"Ms. Tellerico thinks Razi's active body might like the Celia Cruz Performing Arts School better than Langston Hughes. It's a public school, too, but it's on the other side of town, so we have to pay extra for the school bus. Razi is going to try it out tomorrow."

"But he'll be back for the Halloween Parade on Friday, won't he?" Keisha said. Razi had been looking forward to the parade and the line dance in costumes since he'd learned about them in kindergarten.

"Of course. Oh dear." Mama pulled the bills out of the "extra" envelope and counted them again. "It was fine last summer to be an alligator, but now his heart is set on a police officer. Grandma found the badge and the hat at the dollar store, but we need a navy blue shirt." She paused and looked up at Keisha. "Do police officers wear ties?"

"Oh, Mama, that reminds me . . . Mr. Drockmore told us yesterday—"

"Your costume is all finished, Ada. I ironed it this morning. I took up Grandma's long skirt, and I made you a snowy white apron and bonnet. . . ."

Mama paused. Keisha imagined she was seeing her daughter in the full skirt, the snowy white apron and the stupid bonnet. Yuck. If only she could be a Romany girl with Racket by her side. That would be *beyond* Tallahassee.

"Try it on while I walk down to the thrift store and look for a navy blue shirt. Grandma's at the park exercising her toe with Razi and the baby. She wants to be able to fit into the ruby slippers." For months, Grandma had planned to be the Wicked Witch of the East for Halloween. She was the one who wore the ruby slippers *and* the black-and-white-striped tights. The supersecret part was that she planned to wear the emerald ring on her pinky finger for the first time.

"But, Mama—"

"I only have a few minutes. Go try it on. I can make the alterations and hear your poem again when I get back."

Keisha sat down and crossed her arms. *Vera Wang dang-doodle.* How could she tell Mama she wanted a whole different costume on the day before Halloween?

But when she thought about wearing the stupid bonnet, the stupid apron and the stupid skirt during the line dance, how could she not?

Keisha started out the door after Mama and almost ran into Grandma trying to get the baby stroller up the back steps.

"Watch it there!" Grandma said. "The swelling is

just going down." Racket jumped all over Keisha as if she were the most famous movie star in the whole world.

It almost made her smile.

Until she remembered that Wen and Aaliyah and everyone else would be line-dancing in *real* Halloween costumes while she was stuck in the stupid eighteenth century. Blah.

"Heavens to Betsey Johnson," Grandma said. "You look positively mortified."

"Oh, Grandma." Keisha helped Grandma with the stroller and unbuckled the baby. As she held drooly, sleepy baby Paulo against her chest, she all of a sudden felt like crying. "I'm . . . It's just . . ."

"Say no more," Grandma said. "This is serious. Razi, I am going to let you into my Grandpa Henry's war chest."

"Me?" Razi was still. "With the skeleton key?"

"The super-secret key hiding place is my top dresser drawer. And no playing with my silk scarves! You haven't washed your hands."

Razi took off like a shot. Grandma held out her arms for the baby and sat down in her kitchen chair. "Graham crackers," she said. Keisha went to the cupboard and got the box. Grandma put several graham crackers on the table as if she were laying down a hand of Old Maid. Paulo was in ecstasy. Keisha didn't know his mouth was wide enough to gnaw on three whole graham crackers at once.

"Now that the boys are taken care of, honey, tell me all your problems."

"Oh, Grandma . . ." Keisha picked up Racket and rubbed his ears.

When she'd finished telling the story, Grandma said: "Hmmmm . . . if only I were Bohemian." Grandma bit into a graham cracker of her own. "But you know that's not my style. I'm more eclectic."

"That's too bad," Keisha said, though she didn't know what "Bohemian" or "eclectic" meant.

"Still . . ." A smile spread across Grandma's face. "There were the hippie days. I wonder . . . Let me talk to your mama when she gets home, Keisha. I have a feeling we can make this—"

"Well, that was a fool's errand." Daddy came in the back door and opened the refrigerator. "Three interns from the Department of Natural Resources, Bob, myself, Bert, that crazy reporter from *Live at Five* . . . with all the hubbub and commotion, there wasn't even a squirrel in sight, let alone a baby deer. Bert and I agreed we'd go back alone at sunrise tomorrow. . . . Hopefully,

Mindy Patel will still be snoozing under her covers."

"That is all very unfortunate. . . ." Grandma winked at Keisha. "But I know you will find that deer, Fred, because the Carter family never gives up. I'm quite sure of it. In the meantime, I need to take this baby upstairs and track down an old suitcase."

Grandma put Paulo on her hip and left the room, trailing graham cracker crumbs behind her. Keisha watched her father take a fat carrot from the vegetable drawer and slump into his kitchen chair.

"It shouldn't be this hard, Key. I don't get why we keep missing him. . . ."

"We'll find him, Daddy." She got out the list and the drawings she'd made earlier while she was supposed to be doing her math problems. "I think it's time to explore the gray area."

"Again? Didn't you just explore the gray area with the dog . . . the coyote . . . whatever this guy is?"

Keisha held up Racket for some petting from Daddy.

"Hmmm . . ." Daddy munched on his carrot while he studied Keisha's drawings. "A jug of water, canola oil, dried corn, rope from the laundry line . . . oops . . ." He pulled the half-eaten carrot out of his mouth. "You need these carrots?"

"Not every one. You can eat that one."

Daddy pushed the drawing between them. "We used to play this trick in college," he said. "Maybe you better fill in the blanks for me."

Keisha told Daddy what she and Wen had hypothesized about in science class. "I want to mix the canola oil in water and toss it on the baby deer," she said. "That would be easier than catching him. I know it's a long shot, but *if* he gets oily *and* the temperature drops and the plastic gets hard, *then* he just might be able to rub it off himself."

Daddy leaned back in his chair. "Why do I have the feeling I'm going right back to that park?"

"I could do it myself! I could ride my bike and climb the tree. All by myself. Aaliyah says it has to be me to avoid a public-relationship disaster."

"Come over here, Key." Daddy pulled Keisha onto his lap. "What matters most is what we know in here." He put Keisha's hand on his heart. "Not what they report on the five o'clock news. We are a team and that means we solve problems together."

They were quiet a minute, thinking their separate thoughts, before Daddy said, "At the same time, that poor little guy doesn't have much longer. And with the coming cold, these deer are likely to be on the move."

Daddy remembered the camera crew talking about a

press conference as they'd packed up their gear. Mayor Heartwell was going to announce his strategy for making Grand River into a greener city.

"Maybe we'll have the park to ourselves. There's a chance this idea of yours just might work."

"Hey, Mom," Daddy called up the stairs. "Can we borrow your cell phone?"

Grandma appeared at the top of the stairs. She gave Keisha a thumbs-up before taking her cell phone out of its pink leather holder and tossing it down to Daddy. "Be careful," she said. "I just got those Hello Kitty decals."

It was starting to get dark and a little drizzly as they drove down Joan Street . . . not perfect for humans, but perfect for deer. Mr. Gorman was standing on his porch, spreading newspapers over his flowerpots.

Keisha ran over to say hello.

"Just hoping to keep the blooms a little longer by giving them a blanket to protect them from the frost," Mr. Gorman explained. "You got something you need to fry?" he asked, pointing to the big bottle of canola oil Keisha was holding.

She tried to explain her plan to Mr. Gorman. He cocked his head to the side, thinking it through. "It sounds a little wacko to me, but I hope it works. I can't stop thinking about the poor little fella."

Keisha ran ahead of Daddy down the hill to the boardwalk until she found the tree she and Razi had climbed two days earlier, the one that gave her such a great view of all the deer trails.

Setting down her supplies, she climbed the tree, just far enough to get a view of the trails the deer had stomped down on their travels. She chose the widest two and followed them with her eyes until she could see where they came together and crossed. Then she looked for a tree with a sturdy branch that would overhang that spot. Another oak tree was in just the right position. Perfect! With her brown sweatshirt, she would be hidden in the leaves.

Keisha made a path through the brush until she reached the right tree. She could hear Daddy breaking twigs behind her. "This is the one, Daddy." Keisha tried to keep her voice low. It was almost dusk.

"You may have to wait for a while."

"I'm a good waiter."

"That's my girl. Okay, take Grandma's cell phone and call me if you need me. After I hand these things off and we practice like we discussed, I'm going to disappear." Keisha put the laundry line around her shoulders and stepped into Daddy's cupped hands. He boosted her, and she caught hold of a high branch and swung herself up. When Keisha was about fifteen feet above the path, she lowered the line and Daddy started to tie on the items they'd brought. One at a time, she hauled them up, wedging the two plastic jugs in the branches. One was filled with water. The other was filled with a mixture of canola oil and water.

Daddy looked up and waved. They had to work fast so he could get out of there and leave the trail to the deer. He opened the umbrella he'd brought and walked several steps down the path. Then he walked back Keisha's way. Keisha used her jug of water for practice. It took a while before she measured the distance correctly. Too soon and the water hit the ground. Too late, the water hit the ground again. When it was just right, she could hit the umbrella. After they practiced a few times, Daddy spread the corn and carrots out on the trail and left for his spot in the picnic area.

Keisha was alone. She leaned up against the trunk and tried to think waiting thoughts. A crisp fall breeze riffled her hair. Would they go apple picking this weekend? Maybe Grandma would make an apple pancake and they would invite Big Bob over and have hot chocolate. Maybe Daddy would let her use the apple picker *in the tree* this year. And a teething baby brother Paulo would have nice fresh apples for all the sore parts on his gums.

Just as she was thinking about Paulo's gums, Keisha heard a snort and then the thud of hoofbeats. A little fog had crept in, but she could still see two deer coming toward her. No plastic pumpkins. Keisha wondered if she should practice her aim on these healthy deer, but she decided that if she startled them, they might discourage others from coming her way.

All of a sudden, the tune to "I'm So Sexy in My Heels" started playing in her pants pocket. *Jeez Louis Vuitton.* It was Grandma's cell phone! Keisha almost fell out of the tree getting it out. She looked at the caller ID.

Why was Daddy calling her now?

"Daddy!"

"It's Big Bob, Keisha. Your dad told me to call."

"Hi, Big Bob. I'm a little busy right now."

"I know." Big Bob's voice sounded excited. "I'm up a tree in the picnic area with your dad. I brought my bird-watching binoculars. We can see the pumpkin deer and his mama! They're coming your way!"

Keisha was so flustered, she hung up without saying good-bye. She wasn't ready! She tried to jam the cell phone back in her pocket, but she dropped it. It thumped its way through the trees. Oh no. She froze. Now what was she supposed to do? She heard crashing in the forest not far away. Something must have startled the deer, and they were coming her way, bounding along.

Keisha had no practice with bounding! She took the lid off the gallon container and made an experimental pour. If deer were running at twenty miles an hour and water mixed with vegetable oil was traveling at four miles per hour, what time would they meet? *Oh deer!*

Of all the worst things that could happen, Grandma's cell phone went off again. Keisha couldn't tell exactly where it was, but she knew that if she were a deer, she wouldn't want to have anything to do with a man-made noise like that. Here they came. She only had a minute to think. The deer bounded toward the tree. Just as suddenly, they stopped. They must have heard the cell phone. Mama deer stuck her head in the air, sniffing. The baby deer with the pumpkin on its head was right behind.

Later, everyone couldn't believe how she'd kept her cool, but Keisha knew she had really panicked and poured without thinking. The liquid gurgled out of the gallon container, and then—music to her ears—she heard the *plunk, plink, plank* of water hitting plastic. The baby deer took off again, and it was all over in an instant.

Keisha leapt to the ground just as Daddy and Big Bob came rushing up. "What happened?" Big Bob asked.

It was almost dark. Keisha hugged her dad. "Bull's-eye," she said.

After several high-fives, Keisha asked Big Bob: "Will you call Grandma's cell phone one more time? I think it's lost in the leaves."

Chapter 10

"I must say, Keisha, I have never heard one of Phillis Wheatley's poems done to the beat of a tambourine," Mr. Drockmore said, congratulating her on her oral report. "I think Phillis . . . well, I think Phillis would have been moved to hear 'Hymn to Humanity' recited that way."

Everyone guessed that she was a flower child from the sixties, not a Romany girl, but Keisha didn't mind because *she* loved the way her slip-and-slide dance moves looked in Grandma's tie-dye skirt. She went down the fourth-to-fifth hallway as smooth as glass. She leaned with it, rocked with it and finished it off with an old-school percolator move.

"That was fine," Aaliyah told her afterward. She couldn't be too free in her long celebrity dress. Wen couldn't do much, either. She was a colorful box kite with long silk streamers. But Zeke and Zack did their trademark moonwalk-with-the-chicken-head move. Zeke was a refrigerator magnet (all that required was a black shoe box duct-taped to his back) and Zack was a chick magnet (complete with a bunch of his cousin's

Barbie dolls stuck on a silver cardboard horseshoe on the front of his shirt).

All in all, the Fantastic Fifth Graders were . . . well, fantastic.

* * *

On the way home from school, Razi insisted on giving the Bakers' dog a ticket since he was in uniform. Keisha was not in the mood for Razi's shenanigans.

"You can't give him a ticket just for being a dog, Officer Carter," Keisha told her brother. (When he was in costume, Razi wouldn't answer unless you called him by the name of the character he was playing.)

"It's called being a public nuisance," Razi said. "Mrs. Jenkins told us all about it."

That made Keisha smile, wondering how the phrase "public nuisance" had come up. It didn't matter so much now because Razi had had a sparkling day at the Celia Cruz Performing Arts School. After Grandma explained about all the dancing and singing and performing they did there, Keisha was pretty sure Razi would be bouncing up and down in his seat in a new school soon.

"They don't even have a Peaceful Corner, Key," Razi had told her when she went in to kiss him good night the evening before. "I asked."

And now, Razi stood on the other side of the fence while Harvey barked his fool head off, and he didn't seem frightened one bit.

As they came up to their house, Mr. Gorman met them on the sidewalk.

"Happy Halloween, young lady . . . Don't tell me . . . you're a hippie!"

Keisha was pretty much done with the explanations. Whatever anybody thought she was was all right with her. "Hey, Mr. Gorman. Are you coming for a visit?"

Mr. Gorman rubbed his chin and chuckled. He was holding something behind his back. "I think this belongs to you." He held out a dented plastic pumpkin. Keisha's fingers slid along the sides of the pumpkin. It was oily. She poked her hand inside and pulled out a fistful of matted deer fur.

"I can't stay. I'm going to take Tracyanne junior around our neighborhood in the red wagon. She's still recovering from that tonsillectomy.

"I was refilling the bird feeders this morning and I saw this big orange ball—thought it was the neighbor boys' basketball at first." Mr. Gorman took hold of the pumpkin's handle and tugged on it. "But it looks like you really did rescue that little deer. And I thought you should know about it. Those news people, too. I called them as well. If it weren't for your quick thinking, that poor little guy might have starved."

* * *

Two hours later, after celebrating with spice cake, retying Keisha's head scarf and finding Razi's police badge—he'd pinned it on his stuffed bear—the Carters filled their front-door baskets with candy and sat down to vote on what they would reply when kids called out "Trick or treat!" Every year it was different, with some being better than others. Grandma favored weird sayings, like "Bob's your uncle." Razi always voted for the old standby "Smell my feet." Keisha and Daddy preferred something rhyme-y and not as weird as Grandma's. But they'd hardly begun the discussion when Racket interrupted by barking at the front door and then howling as if it were midnight under a full moon.

"That dog does not belong in a house with well-mannered people," Mama said, marching from the kitchen into the hallway. Daddy and Keisha exchanged looks. Was this the end of Racket? Everyone waited for the howling to suddenly stop. Instead, Mama came back holding a moaning Racket.

"Good heavens, there is a *Live at Five* Action Team truck out in the driveway, and they're unloading a very big camera."

Grandma put her hands to her cheeks. "Jumpin' Jimmy Choo," she said. "I don't have my face on."

But Grandma's face wasn't on the news crew's minds. Mama stayed in the kitchen with Racket while

Razi ran to open the door. He rushed out to the porch and said, "Attention, everyone."

The camera operator swung his camera in Razi's direction. "I am the chief of police of this city."

Razi adjusted his hat. The camera operator stopped filming. "Sorry, kid. But we've already got the Halloween footage."

Mindy Patel came up the porch steps. "We're tracking a pumpkin," she said, "and we have reason to believe it's here."

"I have a pumpkin," Razi offered. "But you can only borrow it until tonight's T or T."

"You probably mean this pumpkin." Daddy held out the pumpkin Mr. Gorman had brought over. Mindy Patel and the camera operator examined it closely.

"It smells funny," she said, and passed it to the camera operator.

"Looks like deer fur to me," he said.

Before she knew it, Keisha was hustled out into the last remaining light to film an updated news segment.

After she'd been interviewed, the camera operator said, "We still need a lead-in. If only we had some footage of that deer."

"I am *not* going back there. I'm still picking burs out of my nylons."

"Maybe just a close-up of the pumpkin," the camera guy suggested.

"I could hold it," Razi offered.

"Maybe if he tilted it so we could see the deer fur."

"I know," Razi said. "I could do this." He raised his arms in the air and started snapping his fingers. "Attention, everyone! It's time for . . . salsa!" And he swiggled his hips and waved his arms. It looked a lot like Razi's signature drag-foot-with-the-disco-arms that he did while playing hip-hop-scotch, but Keisha could see that his day at the Celia Cruz Performing Arts School had taught her brother a few new moves.

"Hey . . ." The camera operator elbowed Mindy Patel.

"It has possibilities," Mindy agreed. "Do we have any salsa music?"

"Kid, can you dance with this pumpkin?"

"You bet I can. I can dance with three pumpkins!" Razi turned around and almost smacked the screen door, searching for more pumpkins to impress the camera guy.

"No, no! Just this one. Think of it like your dance partner."

"Who's leading?" Razi asked, holding out the pumpkin. "Me or him?"

"The pumpkin." Mindy Patel took charge. As Razi

step-tapped and twirled in the background, she said: "There's joy at Carters' Urban Rescue today, as an enterprising young lady has freed the little deer—who captured the sympathies of viewers as far away as Taiwan—from the plastic pumpkin whose handle was stuck on his horn buds. The exclusive story, next"—she paused and waved her microphone at Razi—"on *Live at Five*."

Later, bundled in their jackets, the older kids had the last s'more roast of the season before going in to count their candy. Daddy had turned on the spotlights, and with the full moon and the campfire, the yard was bathed in light.

Mama and Daddy, Grandma Alice and Big Bob stood at the edge of the firelight, talking softly. Aaliyah walked over to Keisha. "I know you were in a costume, but for the future . . . don't wear vertical stripes for camera interviews," she said.

"You're twirling your marshmallow way too fast, Aaliyah," Keisha replied. "Mellow out."

"Sorry. Candy buzz. Also remember to look into the camera, not at the reporter. . . . You seem more reliable that way. It wouldn't hurt to have some sound bytes ready, too. You know, to soft-sell the business. . . ."

Keisha wasn't listening too hard to Aaliyah. When would she have to give another TV interview? Instead, she was following Racket with her eyes, watching him play in the dusky brown grass. He seemed to have caught a scent. Mama had told them earlier that Dr. Wendy at the Humane Society would try to find a foster home for Racket—one without any kitty cats—until they knew for sure what coyote traits he possessed. The whole time Mama was talking, she was scratching Racket behind the ears. Even though Mama would never confess it, Keisha thought she liked Racket, too.

Did he *have* to go?

If Keisha had learned anything from this Halloween, it was "serendipity." That was a Grandma word. It meant that things just fell together. Wasn't there something serendipitiful about a coyote dog, a family of urban wildlife rehabilitators . . . and a Romany girl?

"I didn't have one good reason to save these old things, but then again, I just couldn't give them up," Grandma'd said about her suitcase full of hippie clothes. "In fact, I think my eclectic style might be able to embrace some flower child right now."

Keisha watched Racket stalking something at the far end of the yard. What was it? First, he crouched so low his tummy touched the ground. Then his little behind wiggled and he was four feet up in the air.

"Racket is flying," Razi declared from his place by the fire.

Mama had been watching him, too. "I think that rascal is hunting—oh dear, is that our missing bunny?"

Oh no! Racket had his little muzzle clamped around a baby bunny.

Now everyone's attention was on Racket.

"Is that our missing bunny, or is that a snacket for Racket?" Keisha heard Daddy say quietly to Mama. He handed the baby to her and started walking toward the pup. "Here, boy. Here, boy. That's a good dog."

Racket ignored Daddy's calling and made his way over to Mama. He looked up at her, wagged his tail three times and deposited the startled bunny at her feet.

Keisha dropped her marshmallow—stick and all—into the fire and ran over to quickly pick up the little bunny and examine him. There wasn't even one tooth mark.

"Well, on my street?" Daddy said, which was the Carter family response to the "Trick or treat" call this evening. He took the bunny from Keisha. "At least our Racket knows who the alpha dog in this family is."

Mama *tsk-tsk*ed. "The way that dog can fly, we should call him Rocket," she said. "Racket is no name for a pup."

Keisha and Daddy exchanged a wide-eyed look. Mama never named anything.

Mama kneeled down and cupped Racket-Rocket's muzzle in her hand. "You help Razi get over his fear of dogs, you help me know when someone is on the property, you help us find missing animals and you help exercise the humans. I think you will earn your keep. But no dog of mine is allowed to make a racket."

"I like Rocket," Razi said. And to prove it, he put his arms above his head and dashed around the yard. "Zoom! Zoom! To the moon," he cried. Then he stopped. "Grandma, where is my Find-It Man cape?"

"I like Rocket, too," Keisha added. Given a choice, she would have taken a lot longer to think of a name, since names were so important. But right now Keisha was more interested in fast-forwarding to the part where they all agreed on a name so she could breathe a sigh of relief.

"You're serious, Fay?" Daddy looked at Mama, just to be sure.

Mama patted Keisha's head scarf. "You know as well as I do that this child will not be happy until we have a puppy in the family."

"Mom?" Daddy asked Grandma Alice. "Do we have a consensus on the name?"

"Could we consider something more stylish, like Rocky? Or Rocko?"

Daddy and Keisha both wore their pleading looks. They were each afraid Mama might change her mind if she took longer to think it over.

"Oh, all right. It's a consensus." Grandma hugged Big Bob. "Good things do hover around Bob," she said. "Even howling ones."

Keisha went over to her mama and gave her a hug, too. She buried her face in Mama's dress to hide the grin that kept getting wider and wider. The little deer was free and the Carter family finally had a puppy to call their own. Plus she had massive amounts of candy in her pillowcase, even if she had ended up giving half-sies to Razi, who drove her crazy with his begging.

She couldn't think of a happier ending to this day.

Deer Fact File

• White-tailed deer live in every county in Michigan. In fact, they can be found in every region of the United States except the Desert Southwest, Alaska and Hawaii. Adult deer grow to weigh an average of 125 to 225 pounds, and males are usually larger than females. Though their natural life span is about nine years, most deer don't live beyond three years in the wild.

• A male deer is called a buck, a female deer is a doe, and a baby deer is a fawn. A "button buck" or "nubbin buck" is a male fawn, usually six to nine months old by its first winter.

• The top three hazards for deer are hunters, starvation and collisions with cars. To avoid hitting a deer, try to have someone in your car scan the sides of the roads where deer might cross. This is especially important in the early morning and at dusk, when deer are on the move.

• Deer are ruminants. This means they have four stomachs, just like cows, and they graze on a variety of plant material—a hungry deer will eat almost any plant. The only sure way to protect your plants, shrubs and trees is to put a tall fence around them.

• Wild animals belong in the wild. Getting too accustomed to humans, their houses and their food can be very dangerous for them. In Michigan, for example, people hunt deer at certain times of the year, so to protect themselves, deer should stay away.

• While searching for food, deer and other wild animals can get tangled up or caught in all sorts of things. Please become part of the Animal Rescue Team and pick up the trash you see around your neighborhood and parks, and keep your garbage and recycling bins securely fastened.

WHATEVER THE DILEMMA, IF IT'S GOT FUR OR FEATHERS (OR SCALES!), THE CARTERS ARE THE ONES TO CALL!

FROM THE DESK OF
SUE STAUFFACHER

Dear Readers,

Like many of my animal stories, this one is based on a real incident that happened here in the Grand Rapids area in the fall of 2006. A man filmed a young deer with a plastic pumpkin stuck on its head. News reports led to a public discussion about the most compassionate way to handle the situation. People all over the world saw the photos on the Internet and expressed concern. The pumpkin was found five days after the deer was first sighted. (He thoughtfully left tufts of his hair in it so we'd know.) Professionals who worked on the case thought the recent rain and drop in temperatures helped the deer free himself. When plastic freezes, it becomes rigid (like most frozen stuff). That and the slipperiness from the added water helped the deer rub the pumpkin off. But there were no eyewitnesses—this is just the hypothesis.

Of course, we've all been wondering if Keisha would get her puppy, including me and my editor, Nancy. We both wanted her to, but hey! Mama's rules are Mama's rules. I needed to find a way for the Carters to realistically adopt a domestic pet. One day, as I was walking my dog, Sophie, in the park, we met another adorable, friendly dog, named Simon, who, his owner told me, was part coyote. So I began researching coyote-dog crosses, typically called coydogs or dogotes. We decided that if having a puppy helped Mama's family, then it would be okay with Mama. Razi's growing fear of dogs and the need for a good sniffer to find lost animals helped Rocket's case a lot!

If you go to my Web site, you can see two of the photos I used to help me tell this story. As you look at them, I'm sure you'll understand why writers say to each other that a picture is worth a thousand words.

Happy Reading!
—Sue

Acknowledgments

There are two artists whose work has particularly inspired the Animal Rescue Team. The first is Beverly Cleary. From time to time, I reread the books I loved as a kid. Beverly Cleary's stories are filled with gentle humor, great comic timing and vivid scenes and characters. The second is Trina Schart Hyman. More than ten years ago, I fell in love with her illustrations of the folktale *Bearskin.* As Peter Glassman writes, "In her illustrations, we are introduced to a fairy-tale kingdom in which people of different races live, love, work and play together." I share the vision that we all belong to the human race. To see that vision reflected in a children's book was very powerful for me.

About the Author

Sue Stauffacher lives with her husband and sons in a 150-plus-year-old farmhouse in the city of Grand Rapids, Michigan. Over the years, possums, bats, raccoons, mice, squirrels, crows, ducks, woodchucks, chipmunks, voles, skunks, bunnies and a whole bunch of other critters have lived on the property. Though Sue is not a rehabilitator herself, she is passionate about helping kids know what to do when the wild meets the child.

Sue's novels for young readers include *Harry Sue*, *Donutheart* and *Donuthead*, which *Kirkus Reviews* called "touching, funny, and gloriously human" in a starred review. Her most recent picture book, *Nothing but Trouble*, won the NAACP Image Award for Outstanding Children's Literature. Besides writing children's books, Sue is a frequent visitor to schools as a speaker and literacy consultant, drawing on two decades of experience as a journalist, educator and program administrator. To learn more about Sue and her books, visit her on the Web at www.sue stauffacher.com.